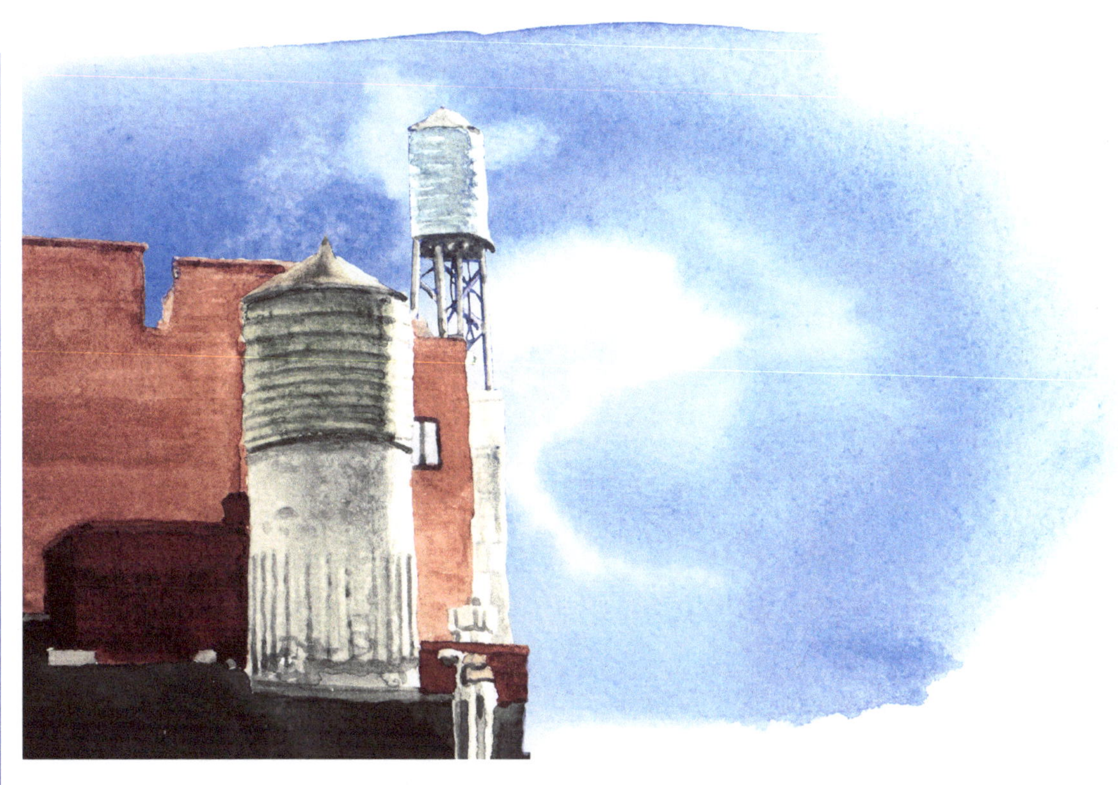

The City Scene from the Sidewalk

Paintings and Reflections from the Streets of New York City

Alex Price

To request permissions, contact the publisher at alexpricecreative@gmail.com

Hardcover ISBN: 978-0-578-72391-4

Library of Congress Control Number: 2020912319

Book design and document composition by Alex Price

The typeface for titles and initial caps is Indigo, licensed from Creative Market
The body copy typeface is Baskerville

Alex Price publisher
385 Grand Street
L 1608
New York, NY 10002-3929

http://alexpricebooks.com

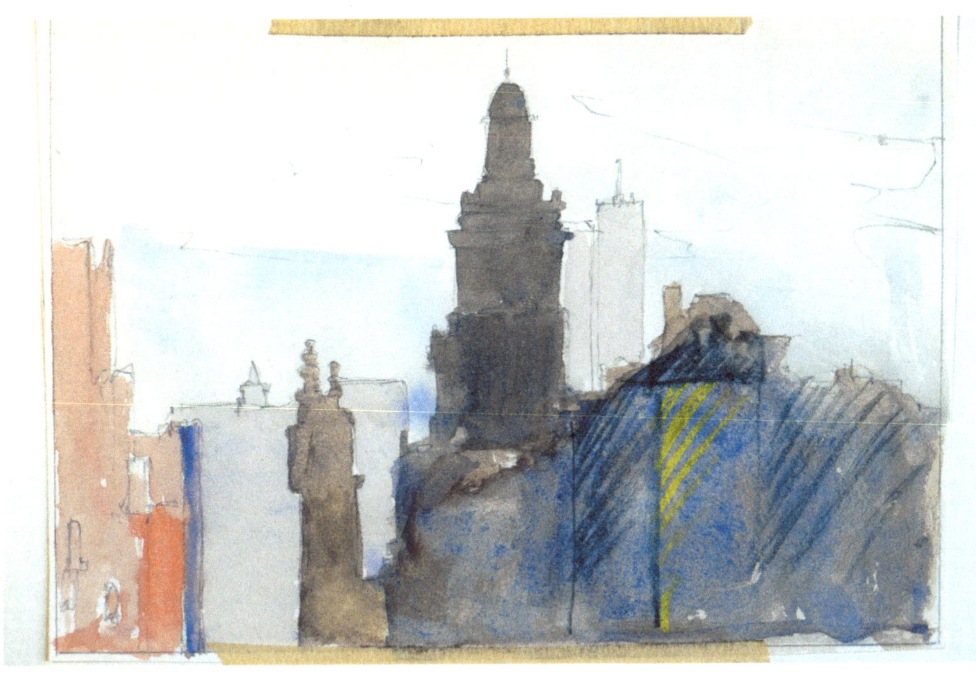

This book is about putting down in paint, pencil and words, my experience of New York City, as an observer and an artist.

As someone who came here to realize a life, this is an acknowledgment of the visual and textural magnificence of this unique place. From windows, streets and sidewalks. From looking and living here many years, this is what I see.

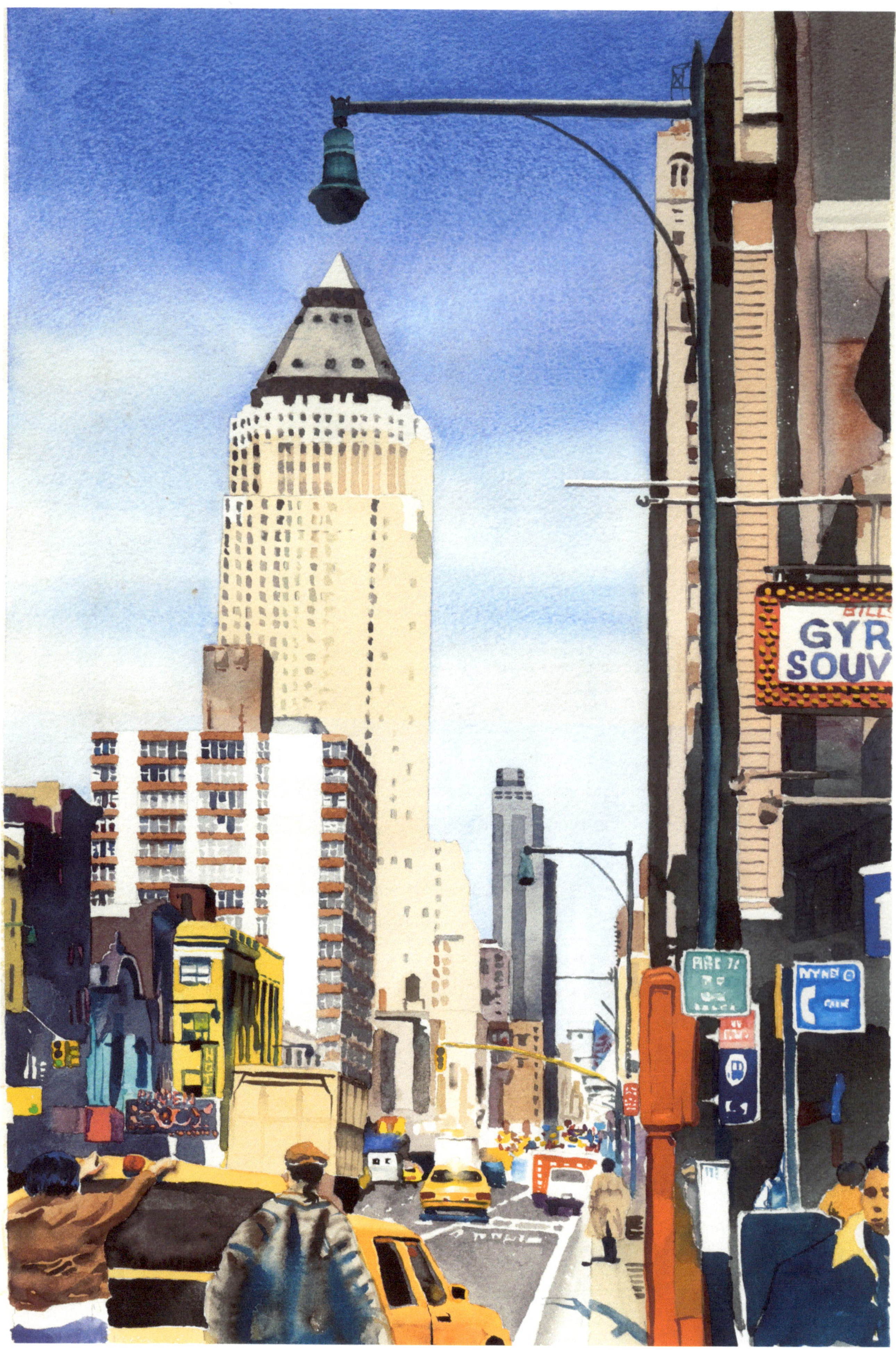
GYR
SOUV

This city, any city, but especially this one, is a methodical maelstrom. I had thrown myself into it out of desperation I suppose. The condensation of people and hustle, along with the buildings, was an escape from the nothing I was used to. It was what I saw and yearned for on TV. Everything was imperative, a mission-critical assignment. After tracing the sidewalks in aimless wonder, all I could do was make it back to my room at the YMCA and try to process what I saw. Later, the exploration of the streets would become an iconic pursuit.

At the airport in 1978, I had just arrived. The weather was rain, overcast and east coast city gray. I had my dad's air force duffel bag packed completely full. By the time I got to Times Square the sky had cleared and I was formally "in the city".

I had stepped out of a landing module onto the ground of a world I had only heard of. This was my first step onto the road that would become my life from then on. It was a relief, I was finally home. I had to find work, attend art school, land a decent apartment, meet people, and start becoming who I should be, whatever that was.

I needed a camera. I had to capture the feeling I could taste by being at the table of this feast. I was coming out of famine, here my plate was full, it was overflowing. Soon I would understand the careful process of nurturing inspiration. It would be slow and painstaking but it would happen.

I would migrate within the churn of this mixing bowl from the 63rd Street Y, to Avenue B and Third Street, and then along an even more tangled trek. Things would settle into a life. These pages are paintings from that life, the visual tableau collected along an odyssey, both arbitrary and intentional.

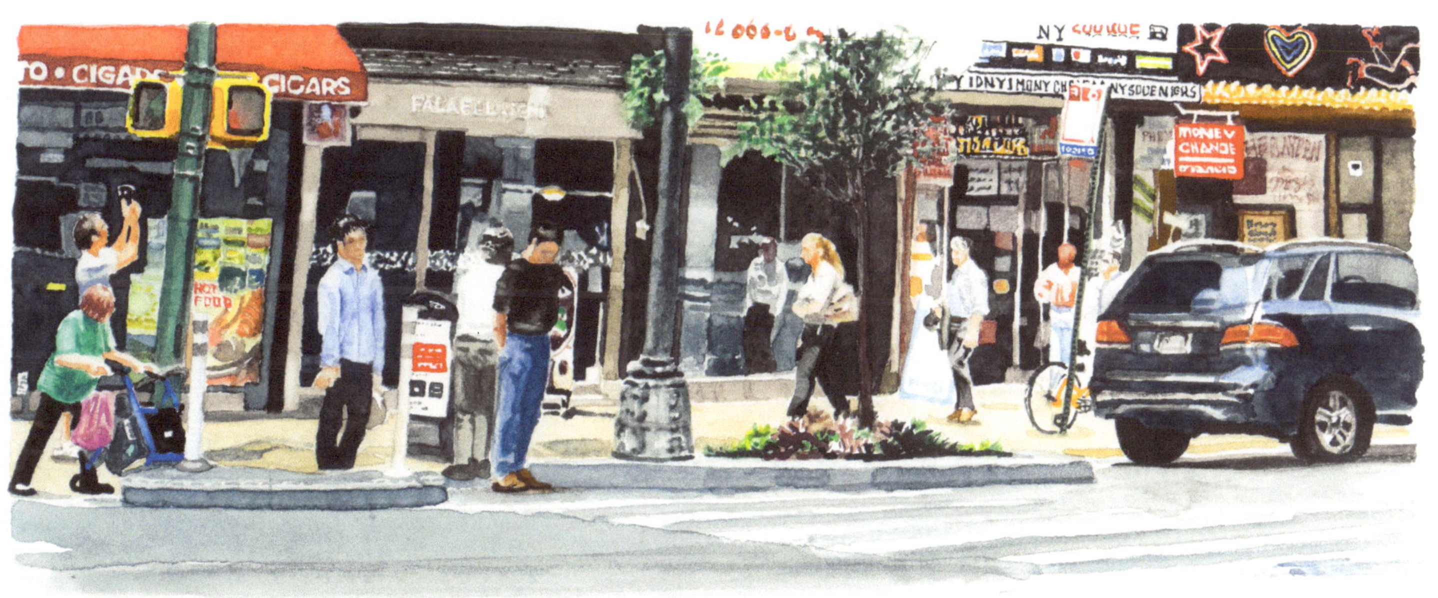

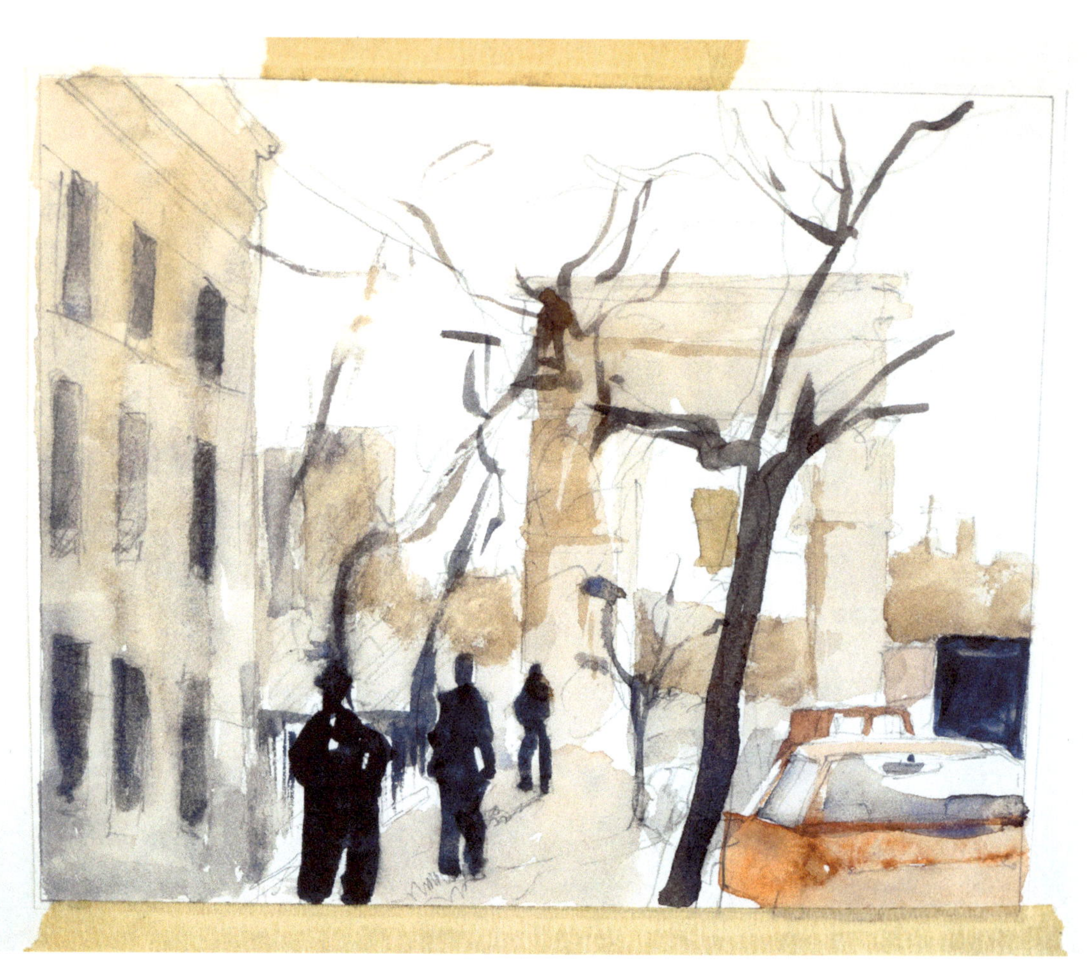

My memories of the early days are always foreshadowing my experience of now. These paintings and sentiments are the records of a sojourn through a distinctive place. What I see, and have seen.

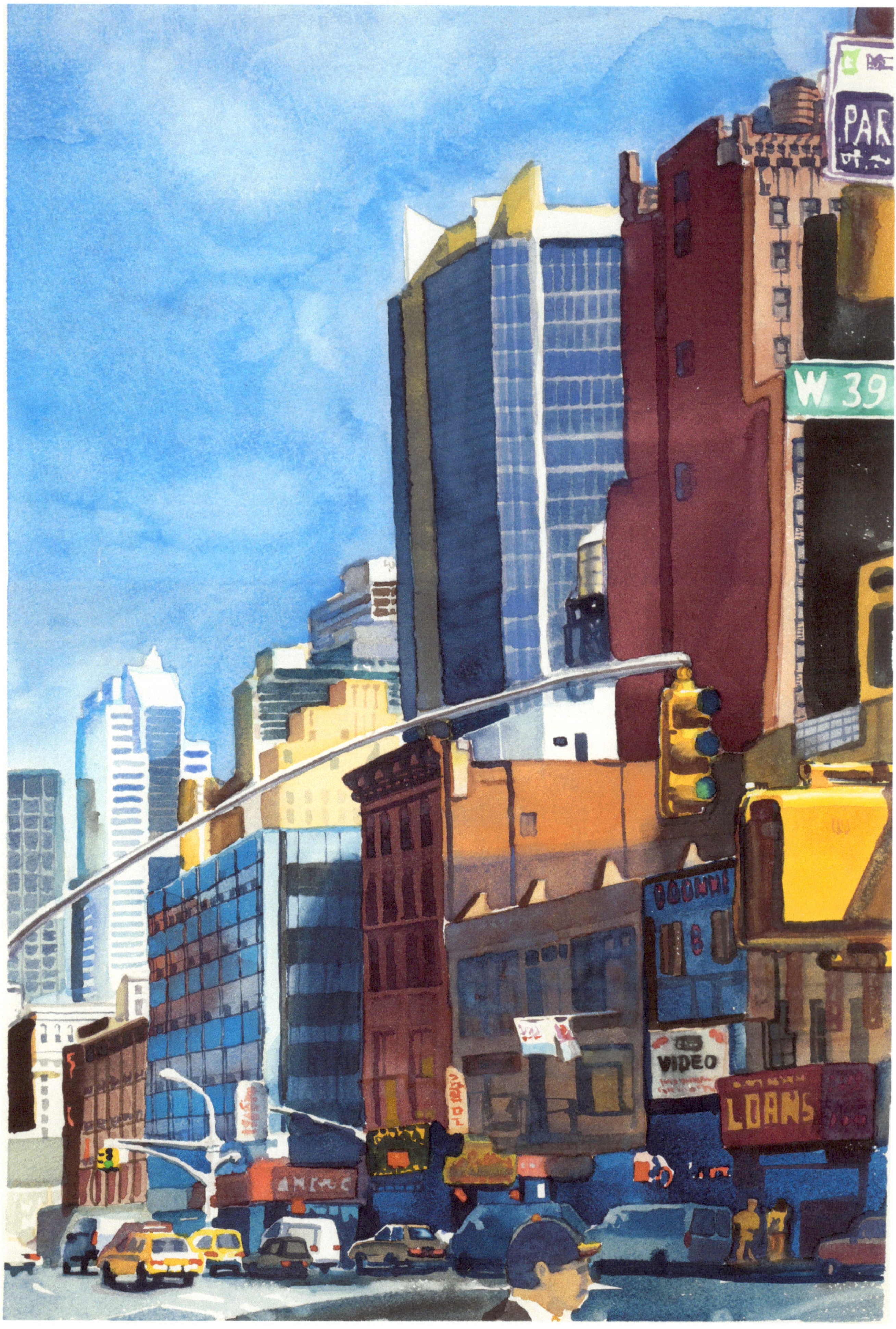
W 39
VIDEO
LOANS

So as it happened on a day of living in a place where I had struggled, where I had made some progress, I saw it as I did for the first time. The impression fell back to 1978, even though it was about 2001. I took a day off to spend wandering with my camera. I had finally scored a career that had legs, some promise, I had been through a few relationships and had a good one at last. The streets sparkled with hope.

This day was intended to recapture the shock and awe of seeing the city after having just stepped off the boat. To walk the street like I did years ago only now having some traction and accomplishment. I looked in windows and at doorways. I was free from anxiety in this encapsulated moment, I looked at everything.

The sky was the same of course, the same as you might see anywhere save for the interruption by spires and top floors of mammoth obelisks. Seeing that shook me back into knowing I was in a remarkable place. Some windows told the story of a temporary residence but the actual space behind the window had a longer history. How many of us have come and gone, the building could be gone soon. Capturing the sun shining on the sill in a painting might be all that will be left of it.

Along with all the glorious majesty, comes malfeasance, graft and avarice. These qualities seem to always play a tug of war in the city. I see myself as a spectator resident, looking through the foliage of tangled virtues and vices. I am also an actor in a production written by circumstance. The grasp I have on all of this is to make a record of the intersections I have crossed and those I intend to.

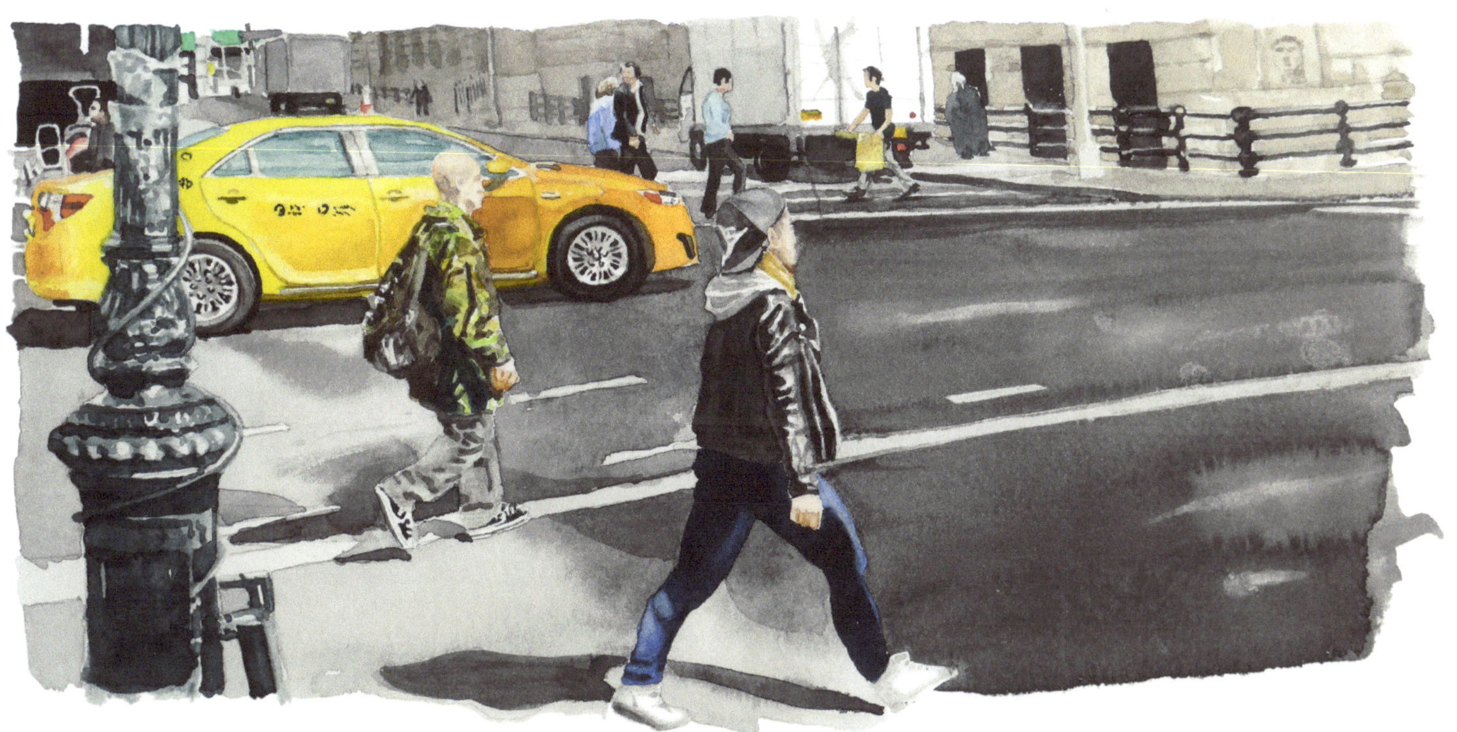

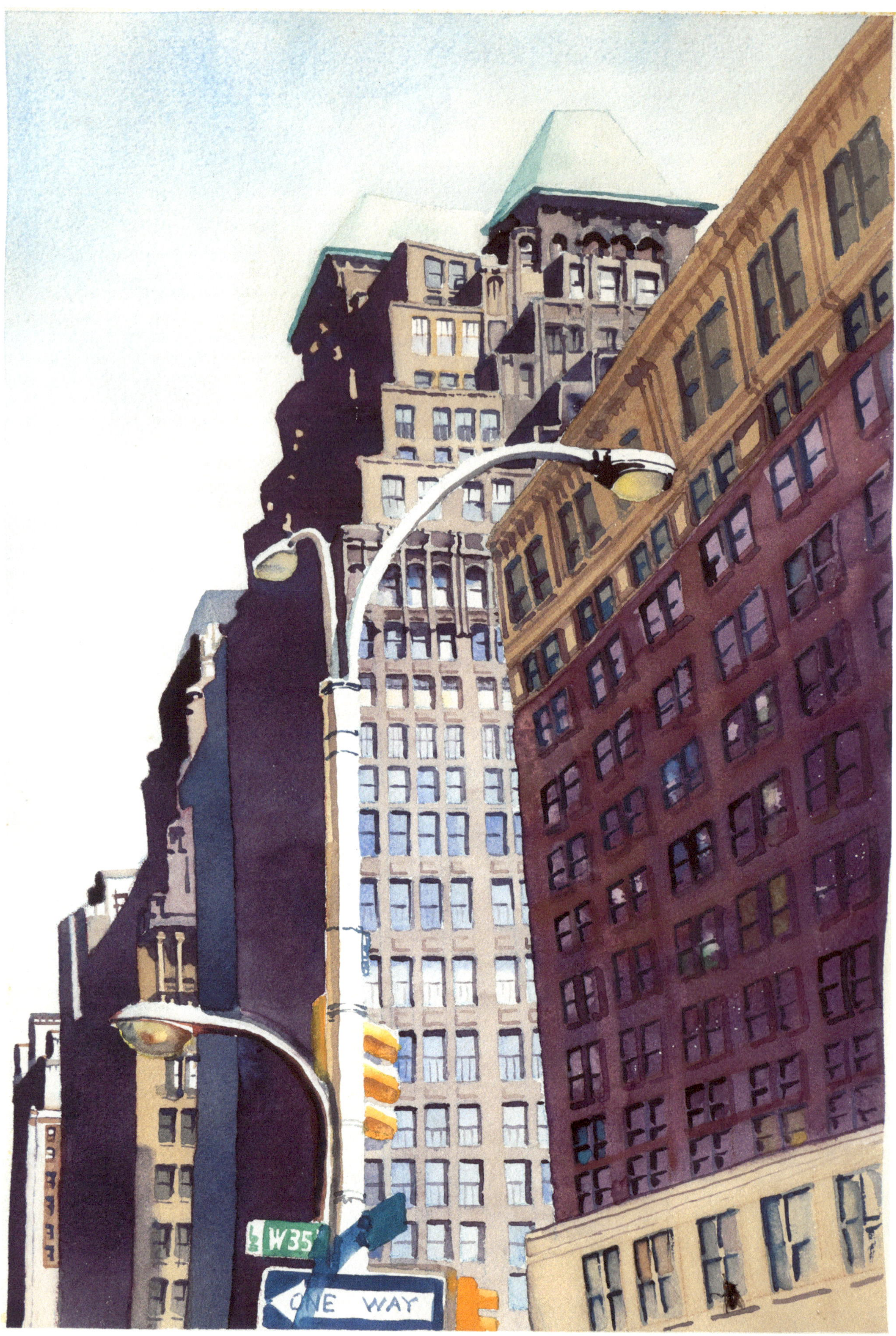
W35
ONE WAY

Looking up as I walk along, I see all these separate and unknown realities going on behind panes of glass, frames and arched lintels. In some cases, the room might be completely empty and I imagine what the passage of time might be like in that space. Dust motes settle into place. Light and shadows slowly make way across the walls in exact accordance with the seasonal position of the sun, relative to the height of the building.

The street lights go on and off according to a timer. Timers control the traffic lights. The sun is a timer. What is the rate of our progress and does anything ever really stop. How long do you have? Well, that would be the number of beats your heart has left. Is there a person behind one of these windows wondering about all this as the seconds tick by?

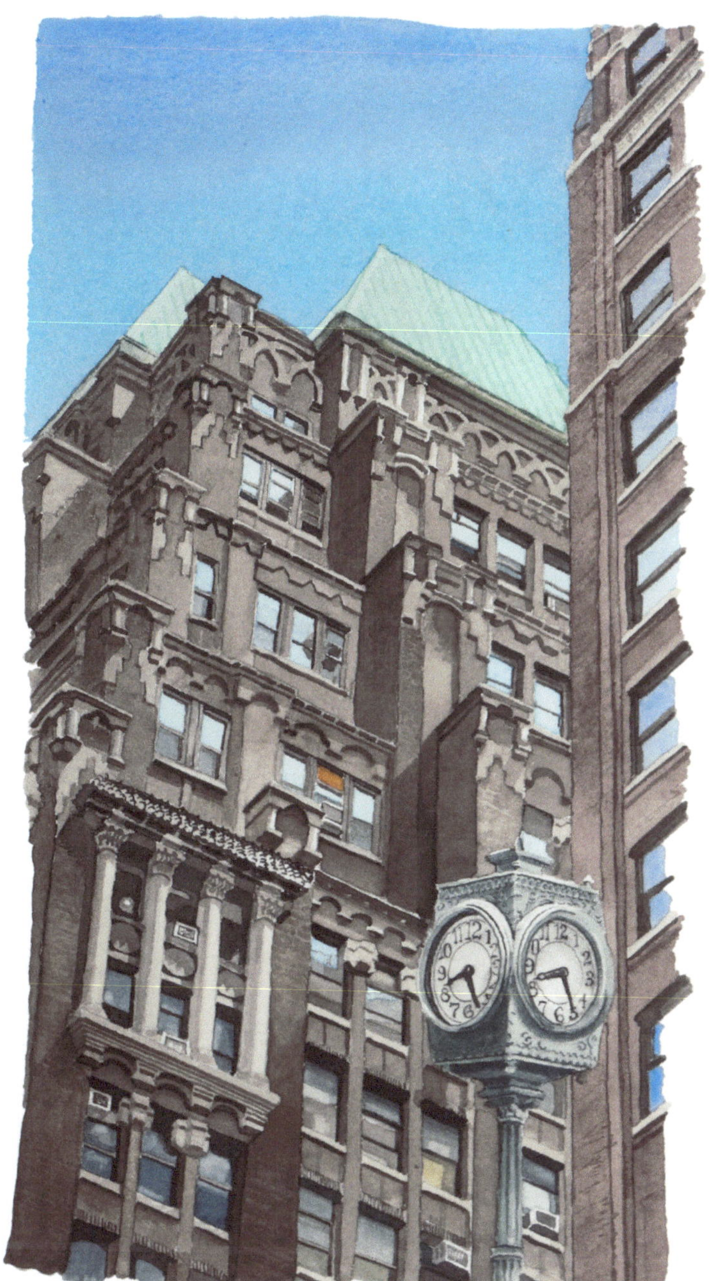

In a painting, one that portrays a scene that is alive and full of light and shadow, you can stop the rotation of the sun long enough to see what's really happening. You can think about things where time is suspended. You can decide what steps to take, then change your mind and take other steps. You can correct what you thought before. You can keep pace with an event. You can breathe. We need paintings because life is fast and unforgiving.

If you are out of breath you have to stop and catch your breath. If you want to make a painting, you can catch a breath and save it for later. For whenever, or forever. You can breathe life back into that moment, then keep it for when you need it. That's one way to stop time.

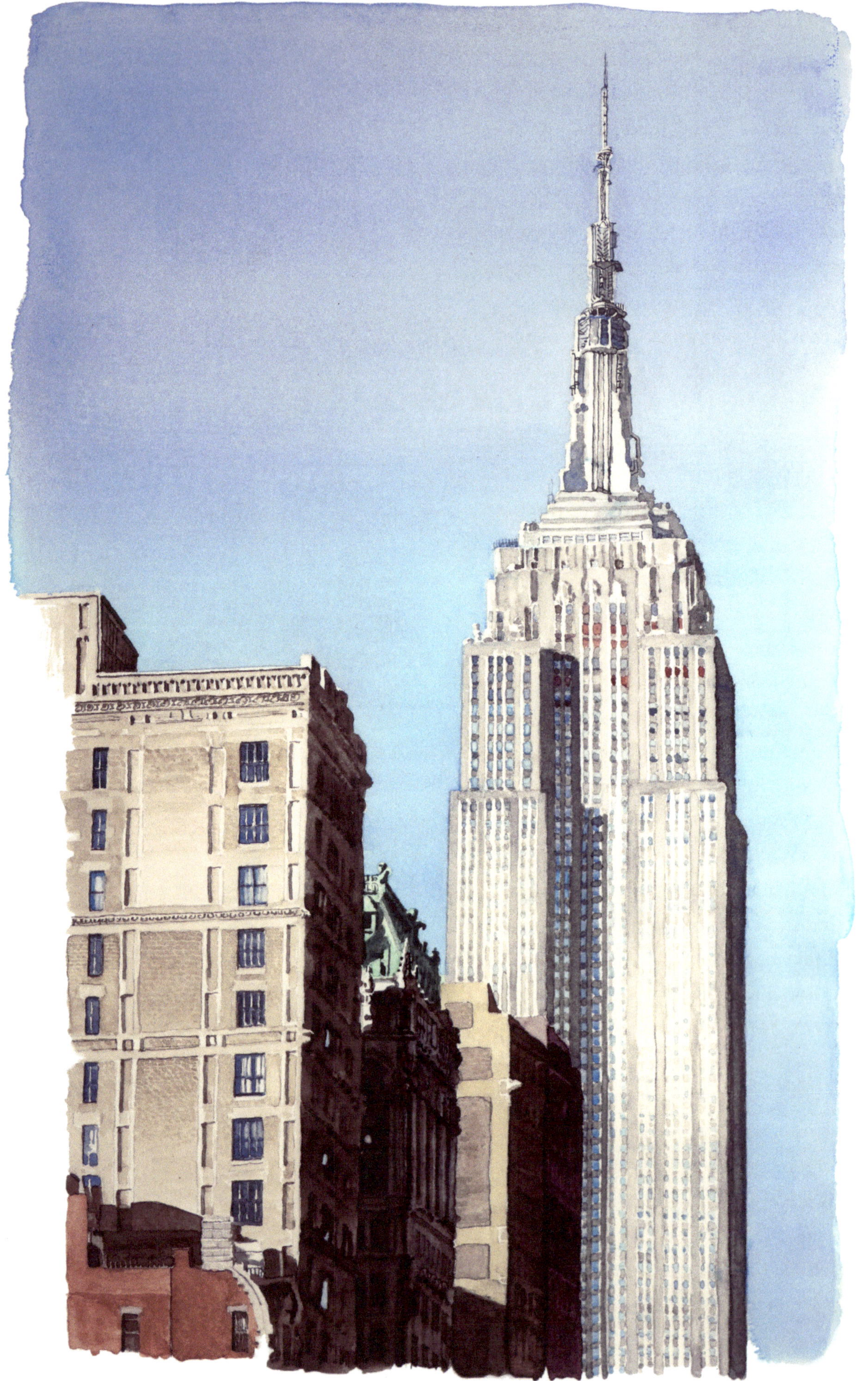

It used to be that you could stand on a high point on Canal Street and look uptown and see the Empire state building. It might still be so, or not, the skyscape is always changing. Buildings are razed, water towers come down, and what was is replaced.

The methods and motivations behind these urban transmutations will always be a kind of vague cynical mystery to me. I'm sure they are based on someone's ability to wield the wedge of urban development. After all, this roughly logical smattering of brick and mortar got here by virtue of this process to begin with. By the way, I'm guessing, but I don't think bricks are used much anymore. I'm thinking some material is stamped out somewhere else then shipped and snapped together according to a plan made by someone who doesn't live here. This would make our new buildings a form of immigrant structure, which is fitting. We might have lost the view of the Empire state building from Canal Street, but I have it here on the right just in case.

There will always be a new view. We go along with things always changing. If I were to give a young person some advice, it might be to learn how to adjust one's expectations without feeling defeated. I am not sure I have ever been able to do this. I want to stop feeling like everything is so arbitrary. Ant hills are built with care and planning, even some brilliant architectural nuances are instinctively deployed from a reservoir of ancient evolution. Then all is crushed by one elephant on its way to the watering hole. This is not even the fault of the elephant, unlike real estate developers who we can blame and vilify.

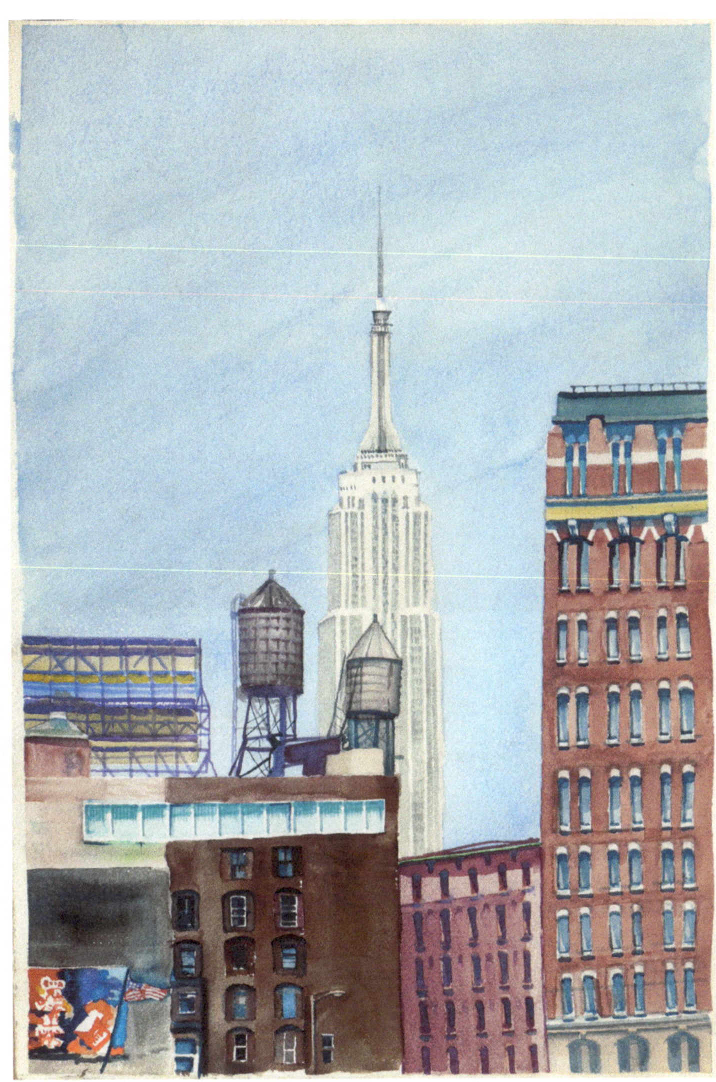

What the painting captures will suffice. Like your memory of yesterday. It's far from perfect and there are things you missed. Unless you write it down (or make a painting) it will probably be lost soon.

Even if you do create a record, the interpretation is up to the interpreter. All you can do is make the record and hold out for someone to experience it. It might not matter in the big picture. My picture is actually quite small, and it does matter if only to me, and you. The big picture is perceived by the small person, then it's not so big which might be the correct way to approach life in general.

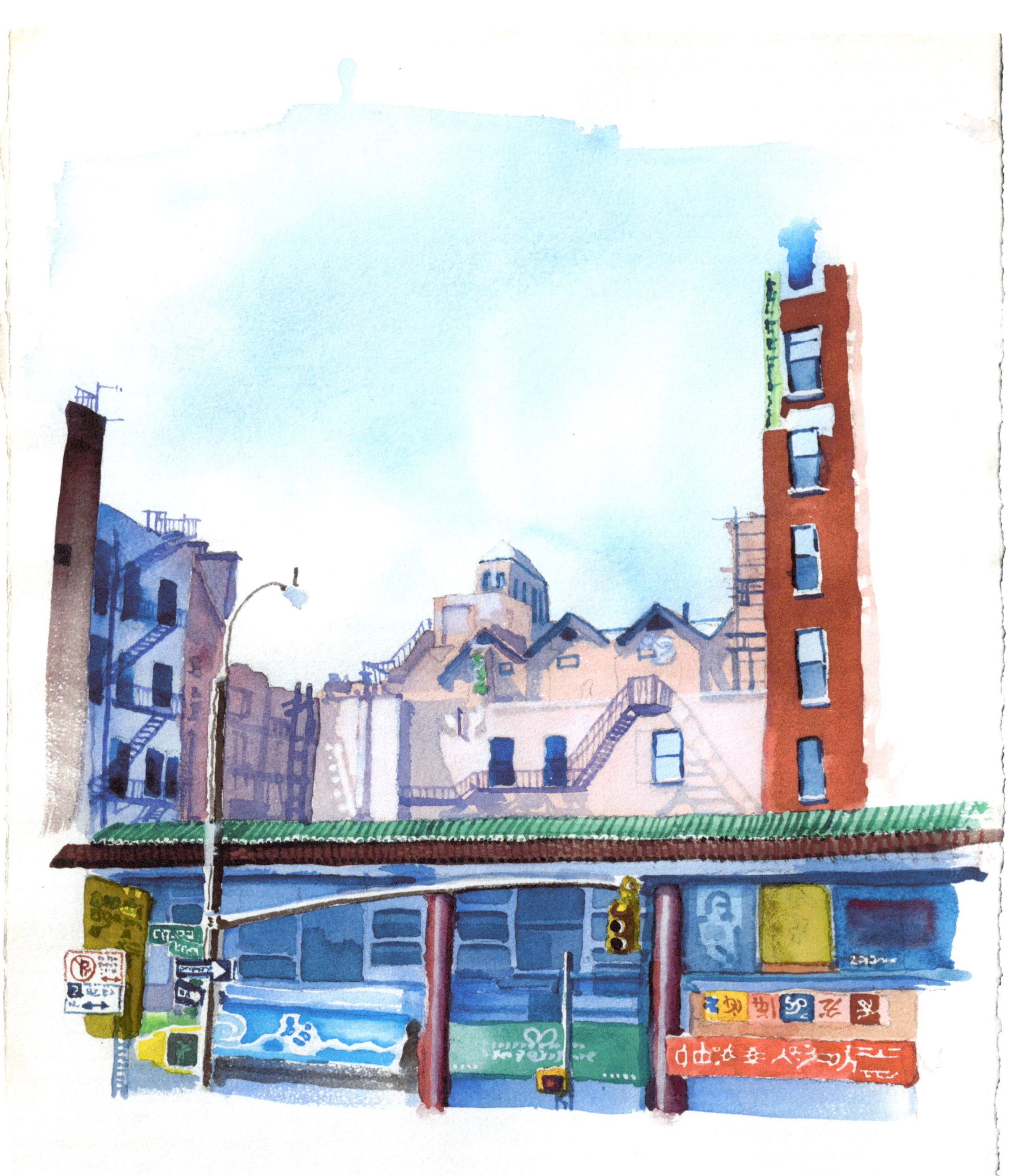

Chinatown occupies a swath of the lower east side. Mott Street is at the heart of it but one interesting street that starts on Rutgers Street and moves into that neighborhood ending on Centre Street is Hester Street. I've seen a lot of change on Hester and some bakeries are no longer there to say the least. This part of town is a good place to float around in especially if you are one of many folks of varied origin. Being a sojourner in this part of town is not unusual. I consider myself an explorer because I came from a world incomprehensibly different. The refuge I was seeking was one where I could be accepted more or less, for being me, whoever that was going to be. I had ideas for that concept and the evolution was happening even as I was standing on the corner of Hester and Centre looking at the shadows made on a pink building by the fire escapes and rooftops.

When I look at the tops of buildings there are often high windows in smaller enclosed segments, isolated vantage places and small rooms above it all. Even the top windows of any building have a certain status for being on top. Our culture is obsessed with being on top. The view is great but you are also conspicuous. When you have something everyone wants, you become an object of conquest. How distracting! A remotely visible place with a great view is better. The room with the low profile from the street may have the most alluring interior. It might be high up but not the highest. Those inconspicuous rooms are where the really important and subtle stuff goes down.

Going into a Chinese shop will give you an opportunity for an aesthetic treat, any ethnic shop will do that of course. For a quick pass into another culture, ethnic shops are the way to see what else is out there. It makes your world more expansive.

If you lived in an inconspicuous room with an unusual view in Chinatown, you might be inspired to stop by a bakery on the way to work. You could have Chinese breakfast, as a guy I used to work with called it. Pork bun, almond cookie, and coffee. He would bring it to me in my dispatch office from Pell Street on his moped. He was from Indonesia. His girlfriend was Vietnamese and they spoke to each other entirely in abbreviated English. I asked him "how do you know what you are really saying?" He shook his head, and said "We know what we are saying."

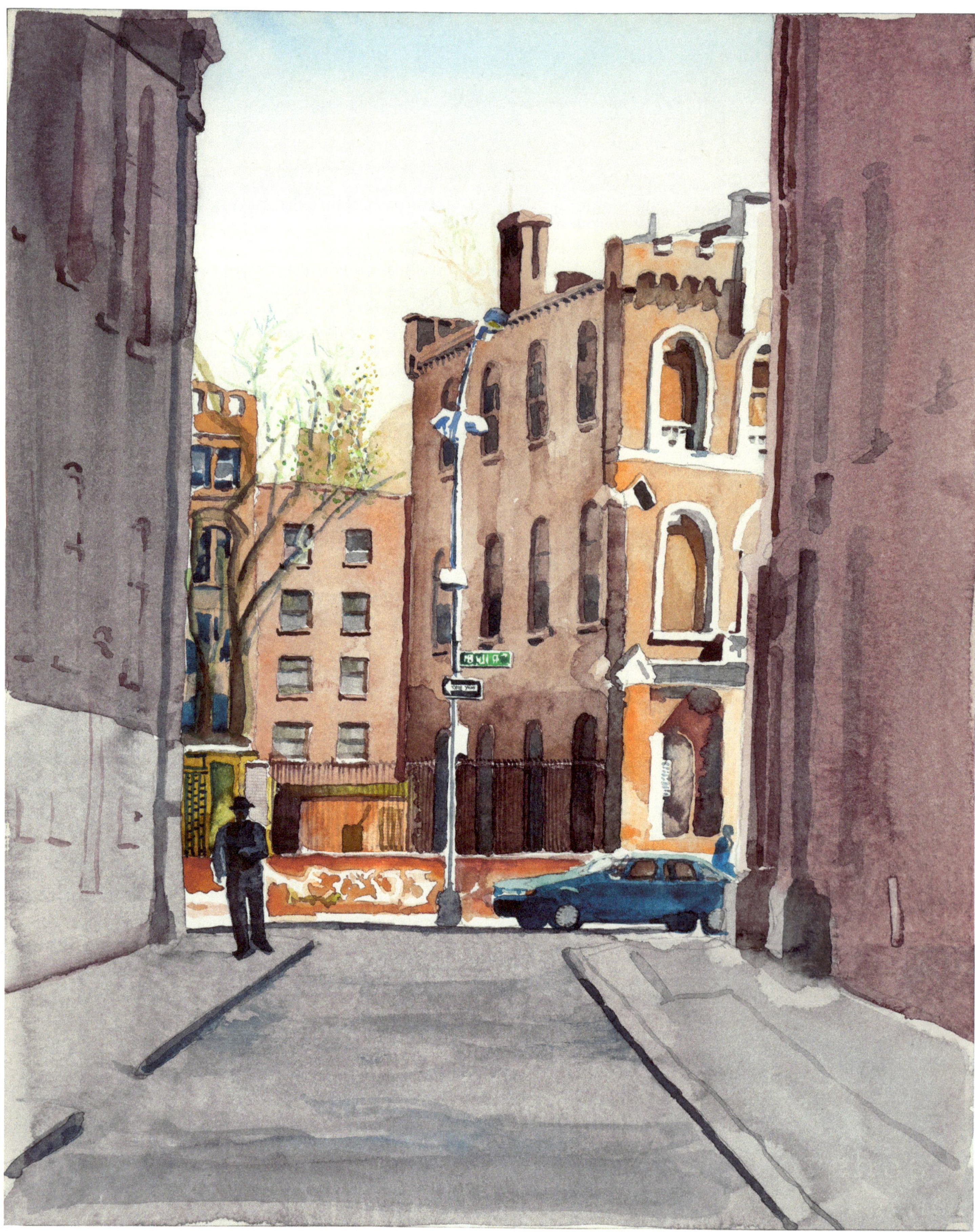

I am captivated by discovering or rediscovering a street that is only a block or two long. There are a lot of them. Jersey Street for instance just below Houston between Mulberry and Crosby. This is a lonely little street mostly in shadow all day and it has a kind of Twilight Zone quality. It's like backstage and it might be the place where Paul Simon says people congregate in shame, but I don't see it as a shameful little alley. It's a place to catch your breath and think about where you are. I see people just walking and thinking by themselves on Jersey Street. You could make a decision between these shaded walls and it would be the right one and later you would remember where you were when you decided what to do.

If you make a panoramic gaze of this little street, you will see a courtyard next to a church just past a wall with graffiti that is always different every time I see it. If you lived in a building on the next street facing the courtyard from your window you would look out on the courtyard, then Jersey Street. One time I was walking past and I saw sheep in the courtyard.

People nowadays can go anywhere, but everyone is still in their head. This is kind of like being sheep in a courtyard. Getting out of your head, is a challenge and I put in a lot of practice and I'm not sure I'm ever doing it.

When I was a teenager I used to go to evangelical churches because I thought they might have an angle on the truth. Anything really true about life, that didn't seem very obvious at the sleepy church my mother made me go to until I was fourteen or fifteen. I would go for long walks on all these dirt roads with my friend Doug after church at night and we would have discussions that almost always turned into arguments. I would always say I wanted to keep an open mind and he would always say that's when my brain falls out. Later I told myself that I wanted my brain to fall out, or at least be more exposed. I wanted to explore the light outside my head.

If your brain fell out on the pavement on Jersey Street, you could pick it up and put it back in and no one would notice. Little streets like this are important for this reason. You can think about anything on Jersey Street. No one is watching. Not even the sheep, if they are still there, which I doubt.

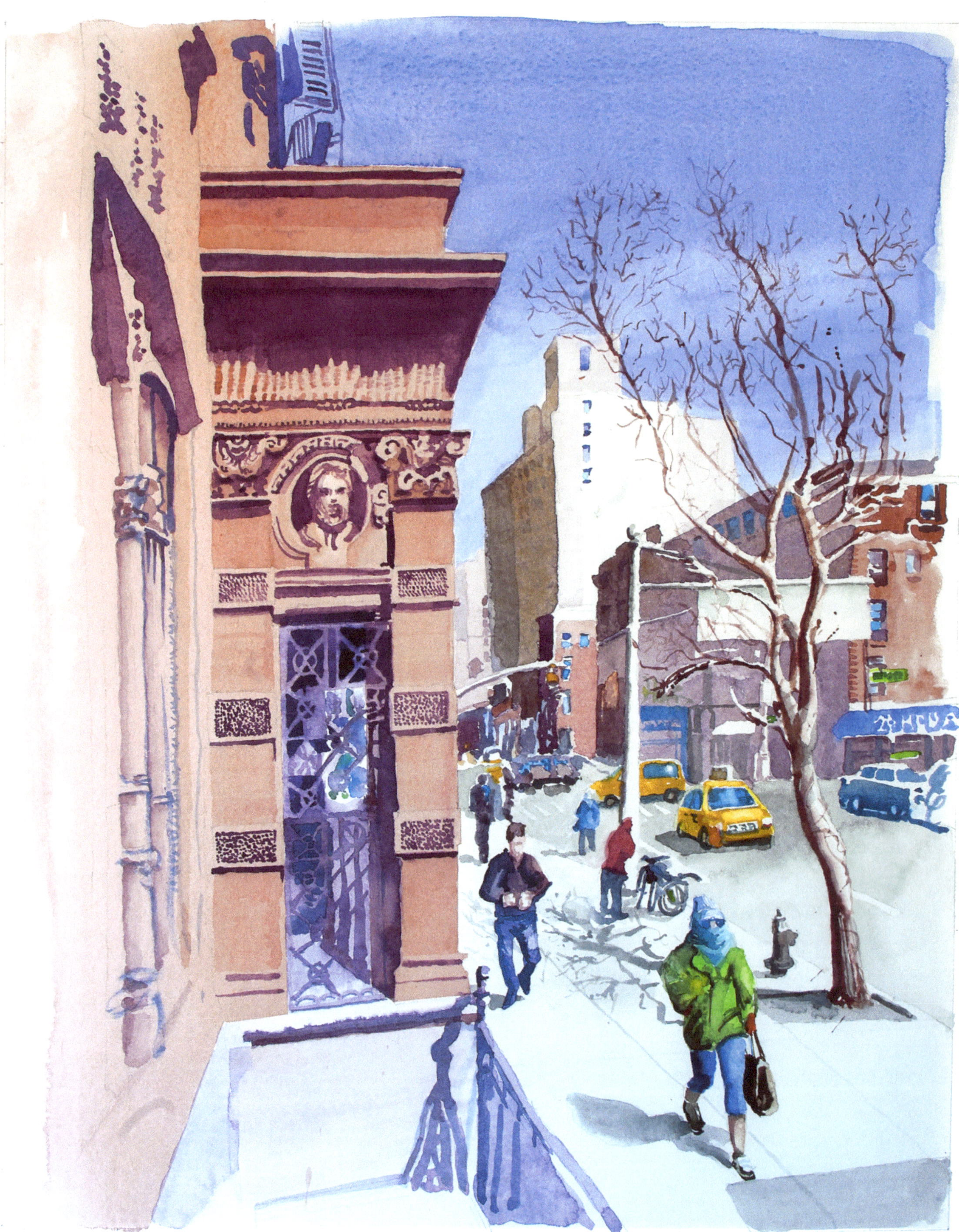

There is a library on Second Avenue. It was the first free public library opened back in 1884 when the neighborhood was called "Little Germany".

Standing on a stoop and looking uptown gives you the feel of the lower east side. On a bright November morning, some folks are in denial about the cold, others are in staunch acknowledgment. The shadows are longer and all activity is brisk. It could be like any other day and you could be going to do something or just out for some air after doing something. The trees in the city are always restricted to little rectangles in the sidewalk unless they get the park. I never know what kind they are, for me they are city trees and it's a special type. (I've read that they are Maple, Ash, even Pear, I've never seen any pears.) They occupy a special space and bring us a unique quality, a quintessential part of the urban tapestry. Dogs love city trees.

I ran into a tree once, when I was walking home late on New Year's eve after celebrating with my friend Robert at our office on 29th Street. Those were the days of early commercial art projects using computers which were expensive and clunky. I say that because now we carry them around in our pockets. At the time, I was happy to have an office and be doing some sort of art, not the esteemed magnificent illustrations I thought I had come here to create, but at least a creative thing with creative problem solving. Navigation is actually a challenge and requires problem solving, or at least directional looking, which I wasn't and I ran into a tree. These things happen suddenly and it's over before you even know it happened. I wondered if the taste of bark was the same as in the country for some reason.

The trees and the light posts, the guys on bikes and the cabs, are statues in a sculpture garden and you can linger and look or keep moving along. The stripes on the street are a language for how to keep moving or when to stop and we need that. If you can make directional lines for yourself it has utility. You can jaywalk but look both ways, or stay in the lines for a while and keep your head up. Running into trees is actually good, it keeps you focused. You might need to change your direction or notice that you've strayed. When I decide on a route to take, sometimes I change to a different street at the last minute. This way, how I get there is off plan but I know where I'm going. Maybe I'll change my mind.

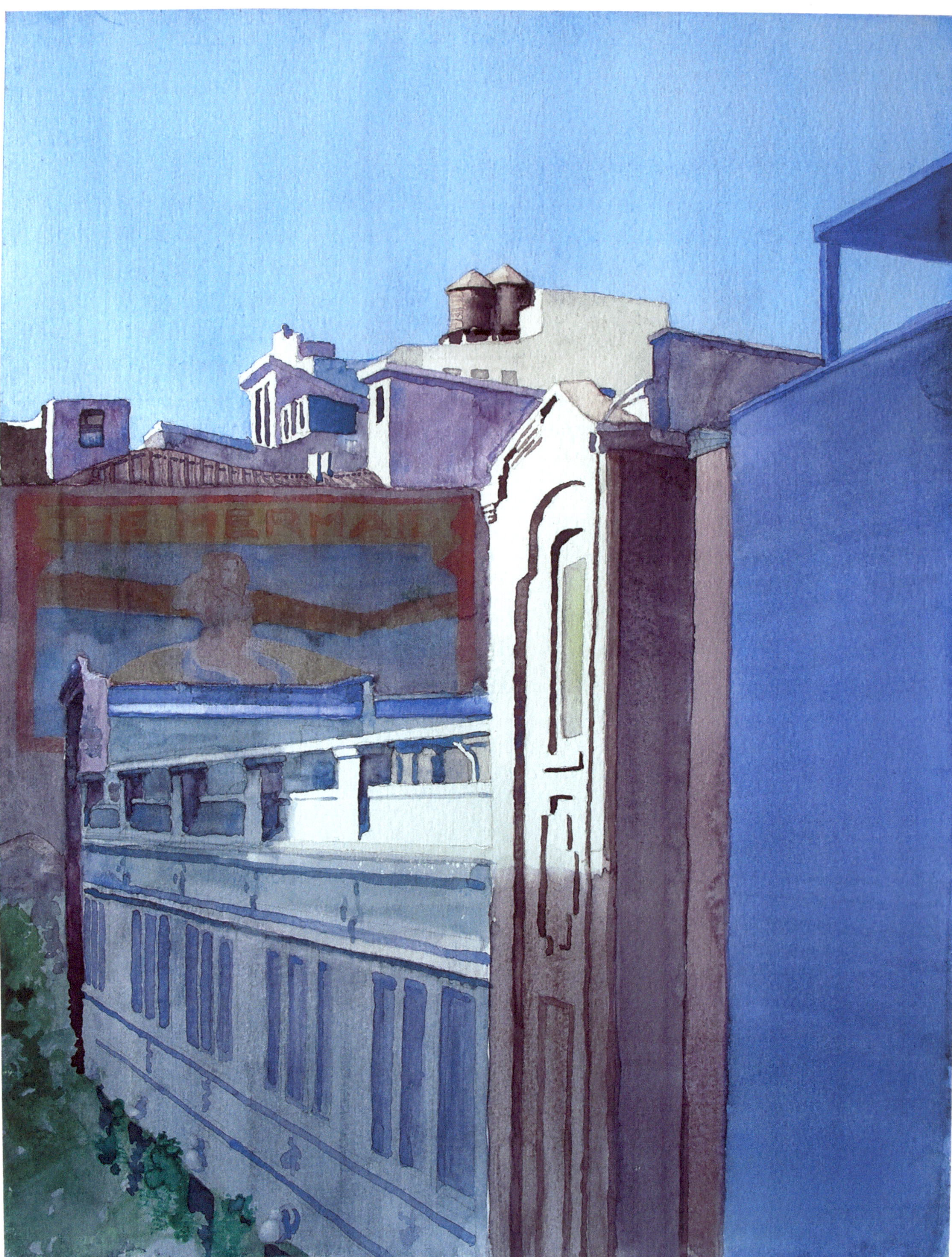

The mermaid isn't there anymore but this moment of light happens once a year at this time. It's slightly different because every year the earth is in a slightly different place in space. This doesn't sound too important, except that every year things are slightly different. This scene has only looked this way for this minute and of course, it's my interpretation which has never actually happened anywhere except in this painting. This painting will be a testament to one small segment of effort based on my observation of my world which I produced during my short stay on earth as a human. There are hand paintings in caves that are based on the same idea. All art is a form of graffiti and we can tag our identity and our personal record however obscure.

In this particular location someone might have looked out their window and seen a billboard with a mermaid then looked again later and it was gone. If we leave a record, a mark, words, pictures, there are several hopes that we might have. A general thought might be that someone else will see it and you will have passed on your impression almost like a short chapter in the story of your life. I paint buildings with windows indicating rooms; indicating someone possibly dwelling therein, or maybe only entering for a short time then leaving. Sometimes I paint things in the room, even the dust. It is that life and that moment with its inherent mystery that I am reporting on.

It is the tale of two water towers and the gravity of their functionality. Images can be sentinels and they promise things, words also. Where the light hits and where it doesn't tells the story of where we live or could live. The way we live. The way we want to live and the way we don't. Someone looking at images created by someone else, is language but the message is mixed up in a data storm of each person's perceptions. I give up defining it. I'm going to put it down and let the message find itself for whoever is watching. I need to be careful, I need to be specific. Within my intense commitment to accuracy is also a commitment to abandon exactness in the process.

We can only control things to a point and when we lose control sometimes it's better, or at least real. This doesn't mean you get to be out of control or careless or irresponsible. It means that we move forward, paint and live with intention and with the precision of thoughtful direction. When the way turns, turn with it.

The water towers are one part of us trying to control everything and one part being open to unanticipated fluctuations in the flow. I suggest an intuitive approach to this balance without hacking out a solid theory and I don't mean a vague approach, I mean a deep feeling approach. Every year the sunlight has a slightly different angle and so must we.

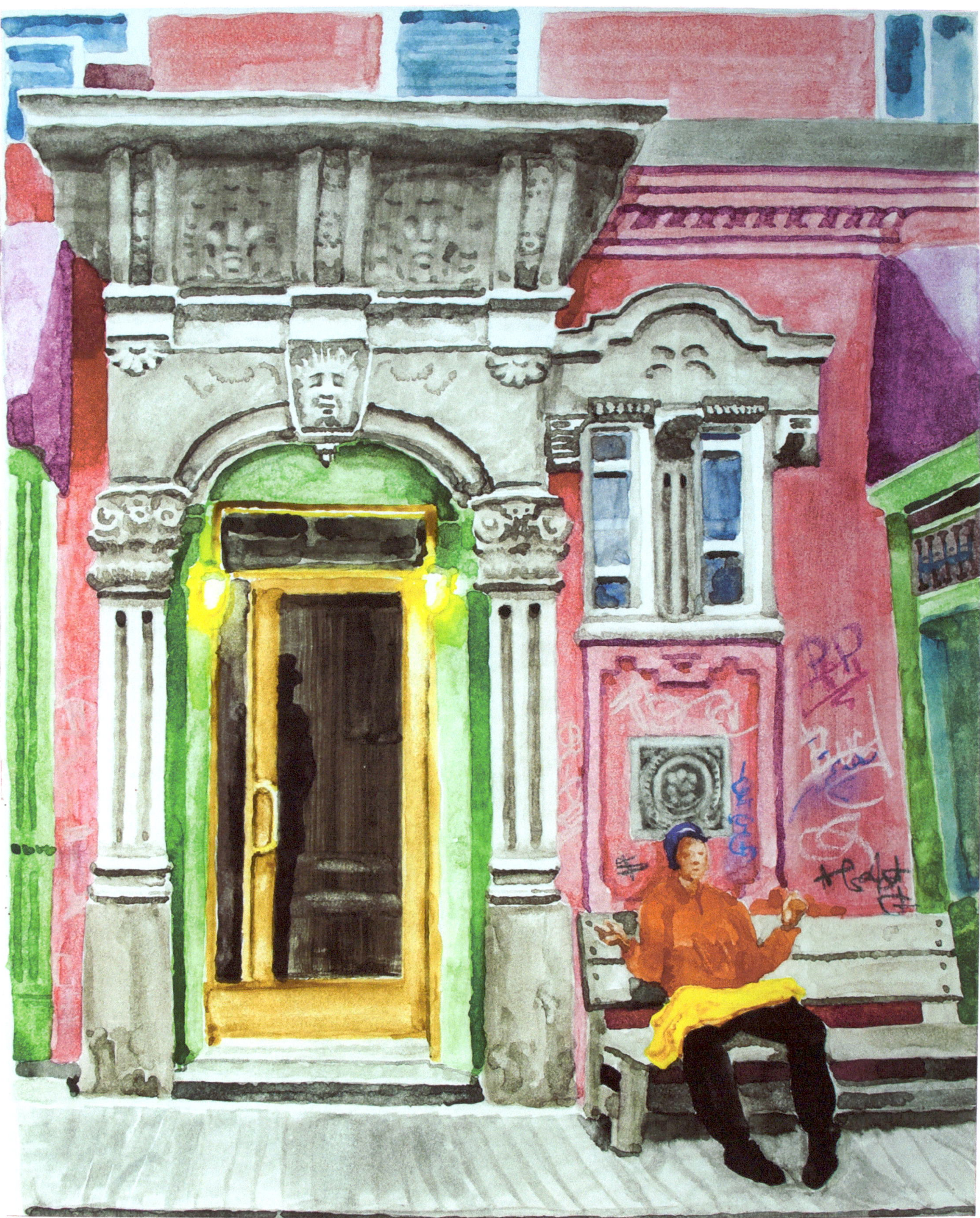

At times, I have found myself sitting on a bench talking to myself and imagining things. I like the fact that it's OK to be weird here. There's weird eccentric and then there's weird weird. Where we draw this line is I suppose a matter of personal discretion. You could choose to be eccentric bordering on weird, and not care, which is what this city is famous for. You really have to find a comfort zone for your weirdness. As weird as you choose to be, know that someone will be watching you. That person's perception and conclusions about your weirdness is actually important because you might need to be taken seriously by someone. Maybe not that person but as a rule you might want to consider adopting a form of weirdness that doesn't compromise your credibility with others. This is actually a bit of behavior modification I have worked on. I gladly pass the challenge on to all artists and people in general.

Being yourself is relative to who you feel like you are today and this may not be who you become. This is one reason I don't understand the logic of having a tattoo. Then there are the voices we all carry around with us, which instruct us on how we should be. I always argue with them. I would discount them entirely except experience shows that sometimes they are right. How can we let our experience inform us on which voice to listen to? Pop psychology attempts an easy answer with "Find your inner voice." Well, to be honest I have a lot of inner voices, it's a warped Greek choir, most of the time I just want them to shut up. What I'm doing these days is turning the volume down low and using what feels like intuition and listening to just that until I get a clear message. It's not always clear but when it's as clear as I can get it under the clamor I go for it.

This process has put me on some questionable pathways, turns in the road I might not ever take should I come upon them again. I feel like I have refined the technique a little.

Painting forces me to walk through this maelstrom in a very overt manner and making decisions is the central challenge. How loose? How tight? How much detail? Which paper, which brush and where is the light coming from. That is pretty much how we trudge along deciding on the material, the medium, and most importantly, where is the light coming from? Using the light to reveal best actions is a nice concept but not helpful when things are dark. A lot of life feels like groping around for the light switch and I have finally decided not to panic, sit still, and think about it before scratching and pawing in the darkness. Things are eventually revealed, your eyes adjust. The switch might not be within hand's reach today, keep reaching.

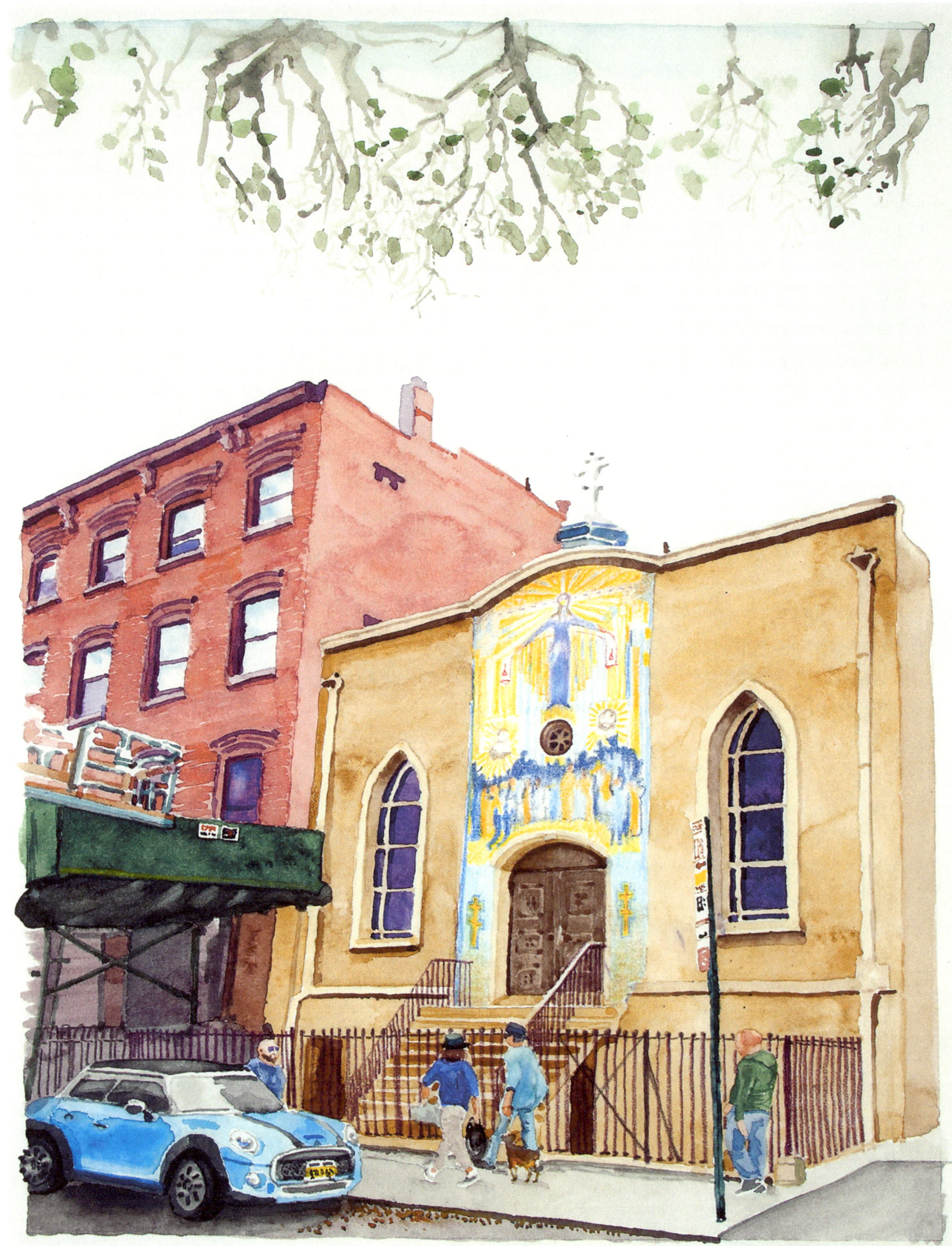

Waking up in the morning in the city and going out to get a bagel is probably something that has great weight as an experience for a lot of us who live here. The day might be hazy with the sky looking like a forever size bed sheet of light celadon gray. If you are near or on east 11th Street you might pass the Ukrainian Orthodox Church, with its amazing mural. Somewhere there will be scaffolding. If the day is gray it has the quality of a waiting room lit by fluorescents. You are waiting for the Sun but who knows where you are in the queue. It's OK you can still do stuff. Remember, arguing with the weather is like arguing with your mother.

When light is diffuse everything is a little flatter. This evens things out a bit and the choices are not as obvious which gives you freedom. This is a time to walk down a street you don't like. There will be things you never saw there and then you can un-like it. Stop in a little store and buy something you don't need unless you always do that, then better not. I have an urge to accumulate things and I question what the point is. Someone I know asks herself if it sparks joy and then how much joy and so on. Having things in your possession can commemorate a certain day or feeling but be careful not to turn your apartment into a swap-meet stall. A gray day is good for sorting things out, maybe even listening to a record you haven't played in 249 years. Do you even have a record player? Ha! I thought not. Go ahead stream it.

This brings me to 11th Street again where there was a record shop nearby that I would drop in and browse. They had CDs back in the day when they were new. No one even vaguely thought that records would go away except as novelty. I still have records and boxes of CDs and I'm waiting for that gray day to play them. Now I tune in to a variety of streaming sites and like all our abundance of media choices the importance of one song is lost in the infinite landscape of choices, most being not what you want. Music is important for when I paint and at this stage of my life, I'm so picky. Old stuff is annoying, new stuff is generic, counterstream inventive stuff is cool but often unlistenable, and I'm stuck with a blend that is apparently referred to as Downtempo Dark Ambient World Trance. This actually illustrates the mood I get into when I need to be both disciplined and creative. What a contrast to the prog rock I used to listen to when I was a teenager. What would I have thought back then when drawing distant landscapes required "Close to the Edge" in the background.

Listening to music while you work makes it easier to float. Floating or drifting with occasional direction is how you get there. At this point, I like drifting into nuance and subtlety. Often a bold stroke is called for but it should be a careful application. Staying within the lines is a challenge and it shouldn't be too crisp. I struggle with how soft or hard the edges should be. It's a matter of perspective and it can be a strain but then after trial and error, it's a relief when things come into that elusive focus. I'm not saying I get there all the time eventually, mostly I'm feeling like I'll never get there. Drifting in and out of my expectations for how things should be, helps to find the unexpected and if it isn't good at least it's fresh.

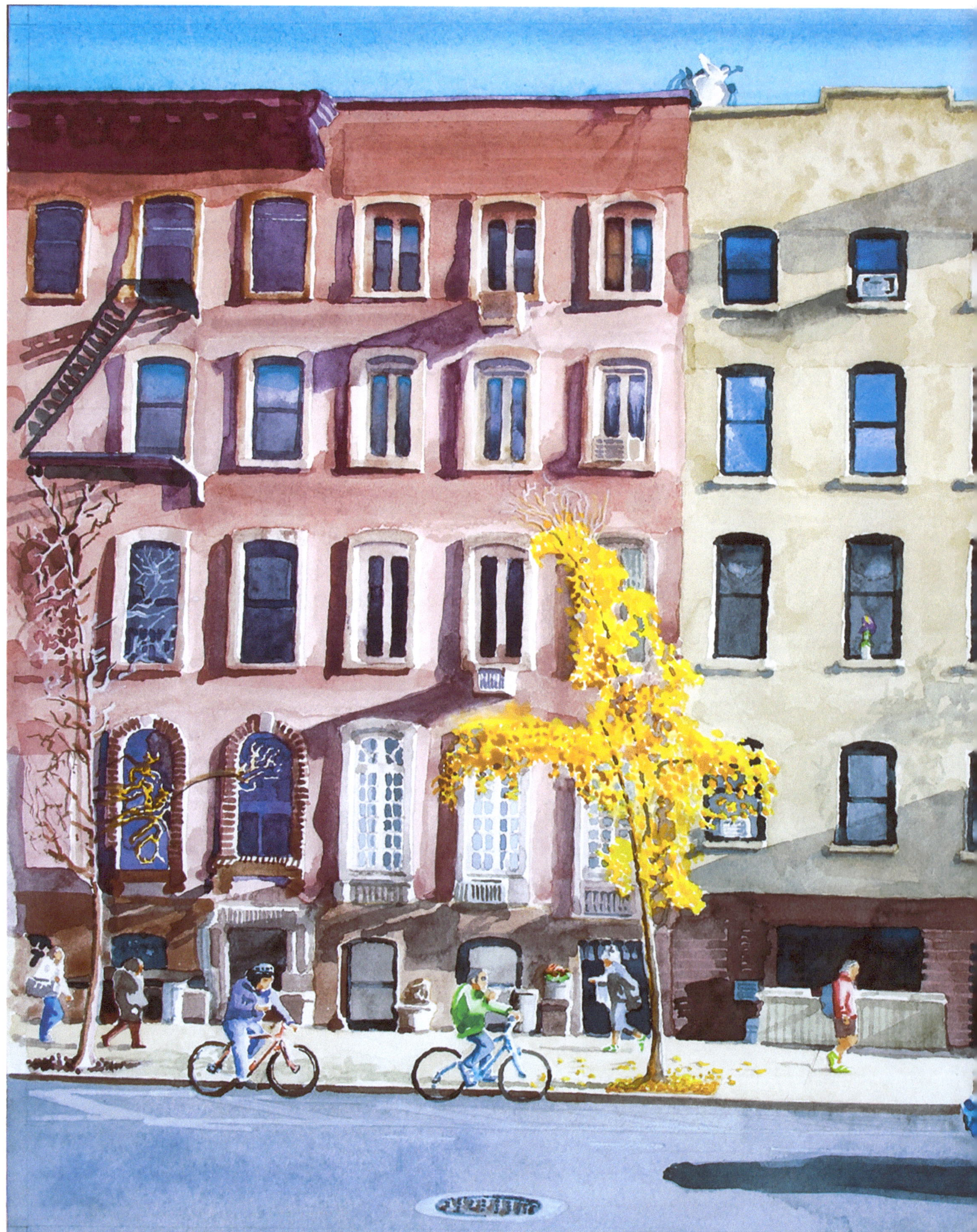

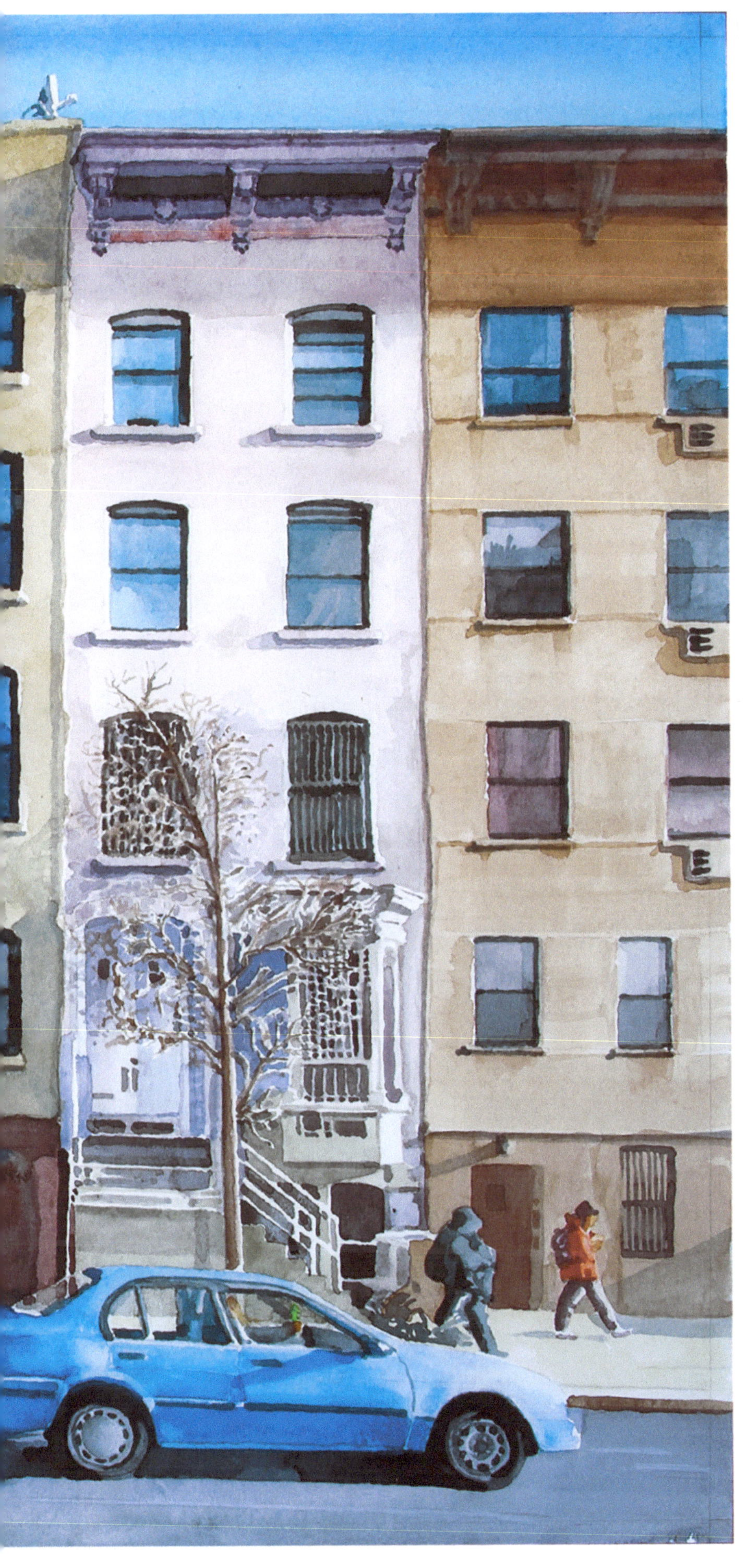

Autumn in the city is distinctive, shadows stretch across everything with long exploratory fingers. It's cool in the shade and hot in the sun which seems to have increased in wattage but moved farther away. Leaves turn color, fall off, and blow around your feet. Trees on Second Avenue around 17th Street turn bright yellow. Everyone is turning around with things and looking back at what and where they have been. Some folks aren't turning around for anything. They will if they have to. Some folks are making or receiving deliveries.

Sometimes not just in the fall, I feel alone in the world even when I'm not. This is because I have a kind of unique experience. One of my secret conflicts. I feel so isolated that I can relate to one lone arctic explorer standing on an iceberg. I have to confess it isn't entirely bad. As a child, I was frequently alone but for some reason it didn't bother me. It was such an effort and disappointment to relate to other kids. Being alone was experiential freedom. Now in the city, I don't feel as alone because there are all these people out there. I don't have to talk to them although I often do for short periods of time. It seems to be enough. The elevator conversation is a favorite of mine and strangely it's like watercolor painting. You have one chance to get the message down and you have to do it immediately with the fewest brush strokes possible. You can't go back, when it's done it's done and you live with it. If you want to achieve anything of value, you can't play it safe and you can't make mistakes. It makes for a kind of fragile, intense, mission-critical endeavor and if you goof you have to start over. Sometimes you can fix it but that can be messy. Sometimes you have to just write off the costly mistake. When it works you either have a stupendous watercolor painting or someone walks out of the elevator shaking their head. No one in my building shakes their head anymore, they are used to me and treat me with tolerance, some are more tolerant than others.

Rooms behind windows are the secrets of the city. Each with its own view and none can be fully understood even from within. Still, there is some comfort because rooms and people are adjacent and share the atmosphere. Cars are like rooms, moving rooms in a vast atmosphere of texture. Then there are the shadows. Shadows define space and within them is reflected light. Ambient light. I have read that on the moon shadows are completely black for lack of atmosphere. So, this means that shadow requires atmosphere to reveal what is within.

The edge of shadow, marking the presence of things, is the transition point. This is the boundary between direct and indirect light. Walking across shadows is mixing the experience of exposure and shelter. We need both and it sets up a certain tension. This combination of extreme and subtle, both existing next to each other, is deep space. It keeps our lives from being flat until we want to lie down flat and sleep. Are there shadows in our dreams? I don't recall any.

Being alone with your perceptions, crossing over shadows into sunlight then into shadow, noticing the textures in and around your atmosphere, is not lonely, it's rich with impression. I want to savor my experience without having to contrast with someone else's. Not as a steady diet, but sometimes. If you know someone who doesn't disrupt your equilibrium you can meet up and explain everything.

Walking over a bridge is something that I love to do, and one bridge among the three that are downtown is the Williamsburg, or Billyburg bridge. Walking over the Billyburg is fun because there is a lot of street art, wacky graffiti, and even some plaintive poetic scribblings that reflect people's need to say something to everyone who passes by without being there themselves.

I have never tagged anything. I respect the need to do so because we live in a world that is so complex that an expression of outrage, insight, or plain ol' personal vanity is called for. It's the name, the "Street brand" that marks territory. It's not just a contemporary form of vandalism, the Vikings did it, the Romans, and of course the Vandals. I guess it's primal, the need to indicate this place where you have been, especially if it's hard to get to. That could be the city in general or someplace with impossible access in the city. I have no idea how some tags get there but there they are and it had to be hard to climb and bring paint cans. Murals are different, they get to use trucks and ladders and they don't have to be sneaky. When I go over the Billyburg, I look for new stuff which runs over the old stuff that's almost washed away. This makes a kind of fluid urban hieroglyph.

Once you cross over, you will find yourself on Bedford Avenue and a block south will put you onto an intersection with Grand Street on the Brooklyn side. Many intersections are sort of tense places. No one can stand in one and look around for long. You have to cross and keep moving, everyone does unless it's a demonstration. There are trucks with mail and trucks with beer. Ancient Egyptians made and drank a lot of beer but for delivery, I'm going to assume they used camels. I think that at least at one point in Mesopotamia there was a crossing of roadways and a single person paused for a moment on their camel and gazed at a temple or holy structure and thought about stopping for a beer later. The island between streets is a place for those lonely city trees perched on the banks of traffic rivers, they seem stark but green nonetheless.

Outside the city, just outside, just over a bridge, any bridge, things thin out and spread out. The landscape isn't as dense and there is more sky. Every once in a while you can still see a shining domed structure with trucks streaming by. The pedestrian, the observer, forges a way on and off the sidewalk taking it all in on the fly.

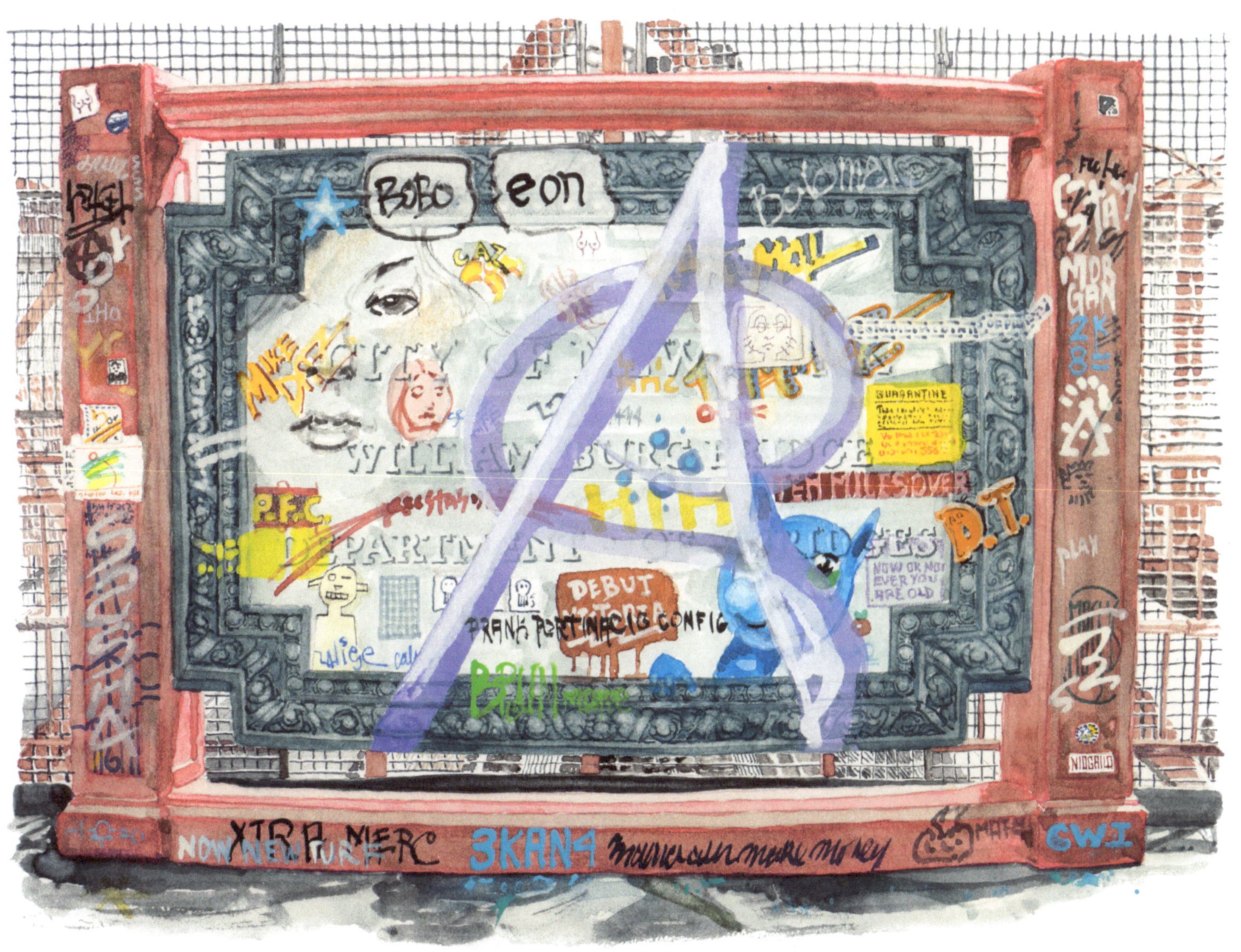

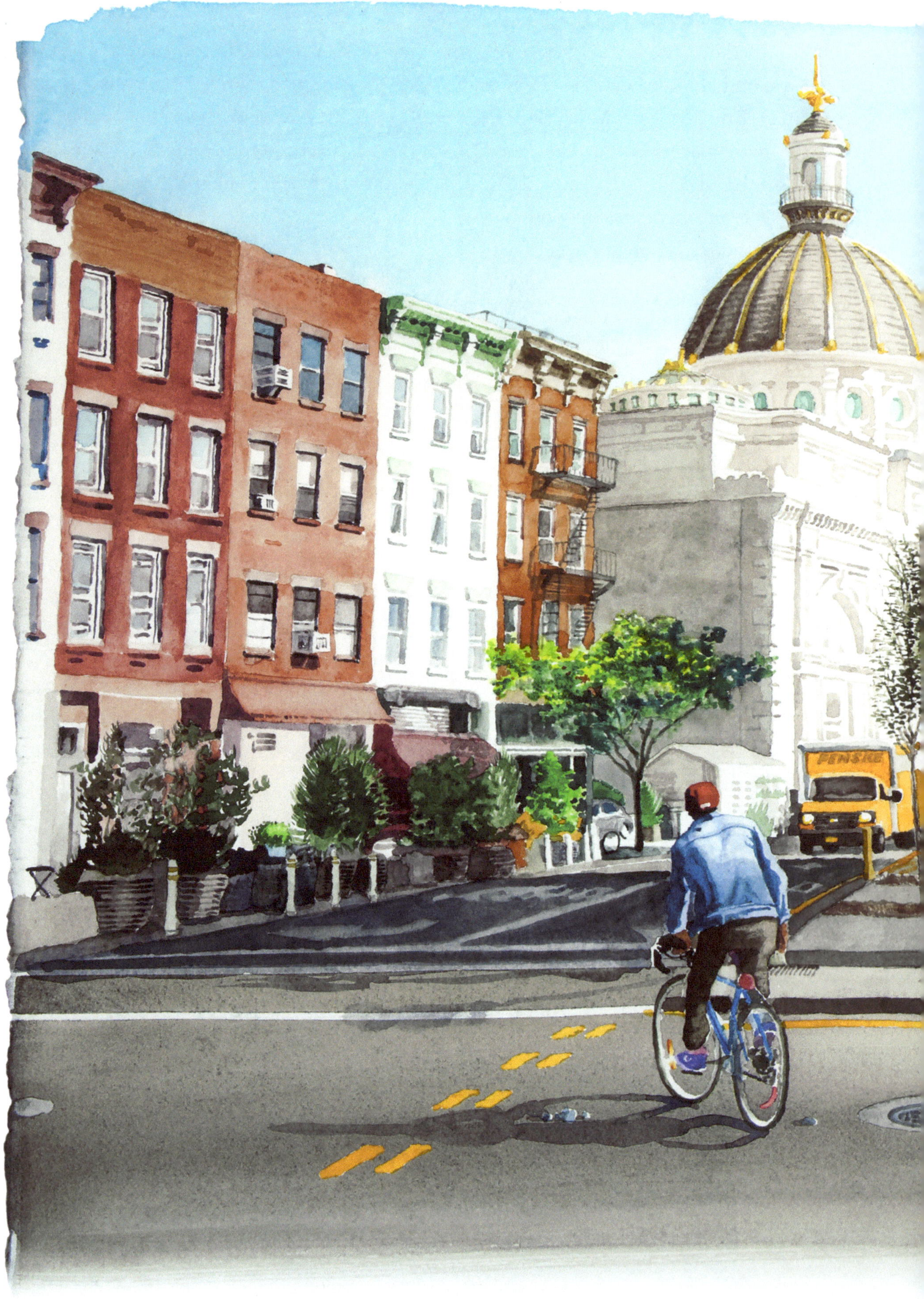
PENSKE

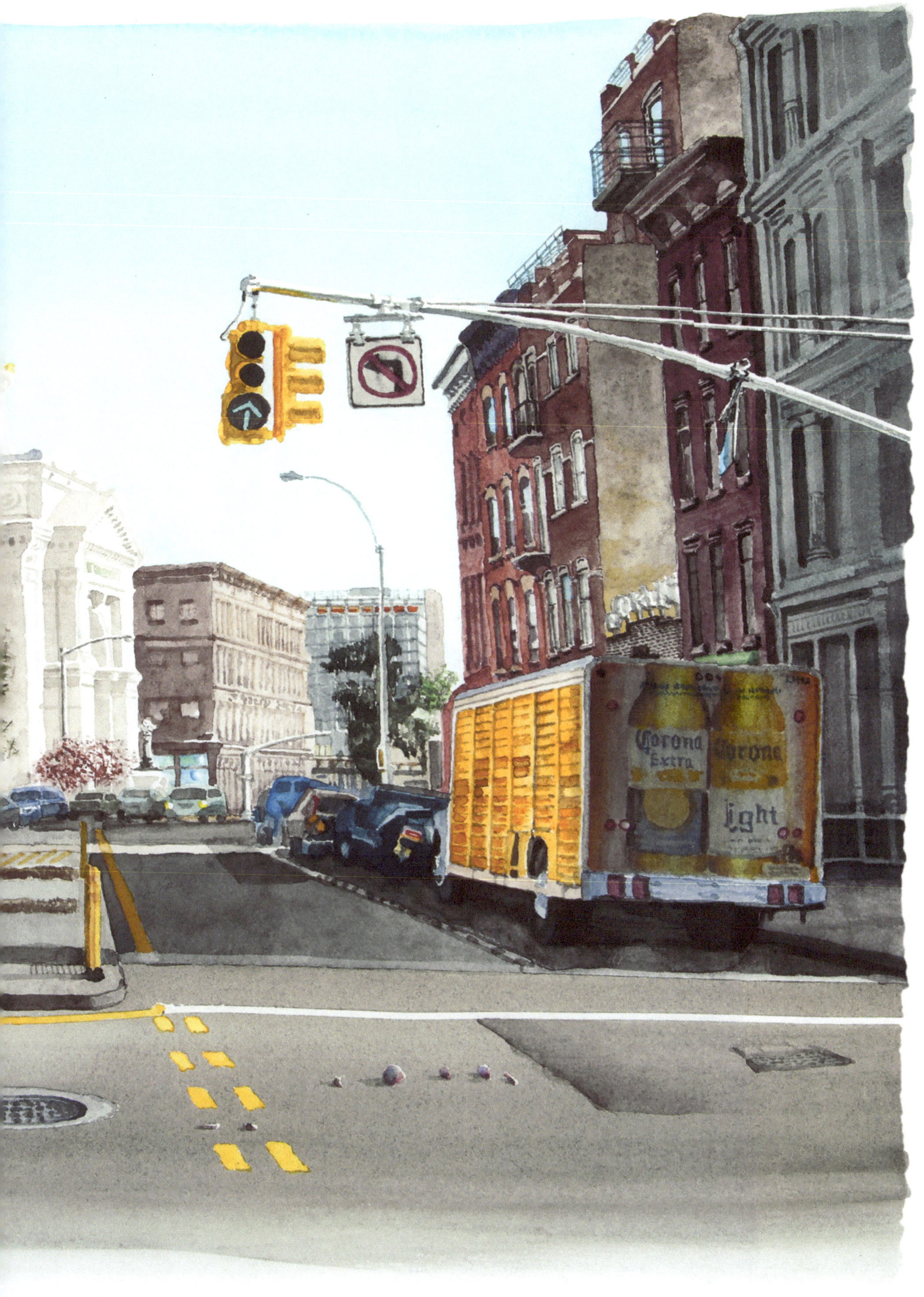
Corona
Extra
Corona
Light

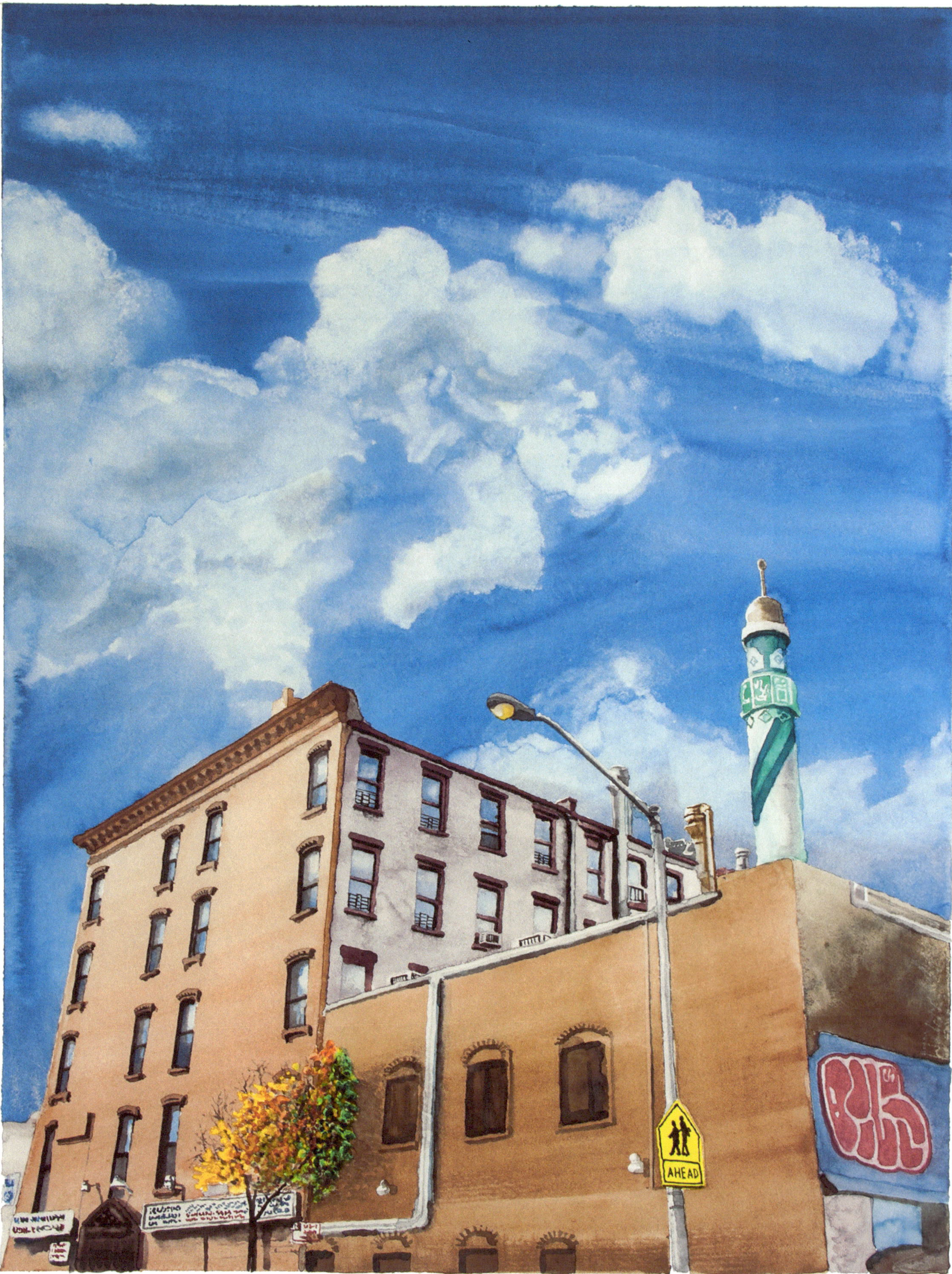
AHEAD

There are many towers in the city. There is a mosque on the lower east side and it has a minaret rising out of buildings seen from the street. I saw it once against an ambitious sky and it looked proud and soulful. The afternoon light gave the scene its usual pensive persona. I'm not religious however I am extremely religious. I am not a devotee of any religion yet my devotion is intensely committed. I don't pray but I have deep feelings that sometimes feel like prayer. I don't believe in any particular higher power but I endeavor to empower myself with perspective and awareness. The gold dome atop this minaret is like the Arabic translation of minaret, it is a beacon. It stands out, shining in the sun like so many towers here. I'm not one for standing out and shining in the sun per se, but I will acknowledge the virtue of a sentinel in a landscape. It can symbolize one's hope to see a higher or brighter truth when all around you is vague and maddeningly subjective. There is some truth about one thing or another to be had if you look for it but most likely it's also changing like the leaves in September. I stay committed to what I really know, remain loose about the long list of things I don't and when I'm walking in the city, I look up for inspiration. Frequently.

Then there are the windows and the hieroglyphs. The signs. The signs tell us what's coming and going and when to walk. Also, the sky all around us is reflected in the windows which means the mysteries and interiors of things we can't see are behind a reflection. What I want to paint, is a reflection of what is really there. I want to enter the room, I think I know what's there, but it turns out different or completely not what I expected, which is good. I don't want to predetermine every step because then it's not an adventure. This means I have to be ready for anything, which is often a disappointment. It's OK because the parts I have seen will help navigate the parts I haven't.

When a street light is turned on and it's still light out, some municipal timing system is a little off. Exact time is relentless and horribly unforgiving. Yet, everything is tied to a certain time and we obey the rules. Our timing might be off, but we are happy if we are on time anyway. I both worry about it and try not to, allowing for an acceptable margin for error. Easier said than done, I know.

The signs are both incidental and important, timing seems to rule all things, but inspiration and hope gather unpredictably. When they come together unexpectedly, you could call it kismet (destiny). This is a Turkish word, from the Arabic *qisma* (portion). This might mean that inspiration and hope are inevitably portioned out at key moments when least expected. That's why I'm always looking, especially when the clouds are determined and ambitious.

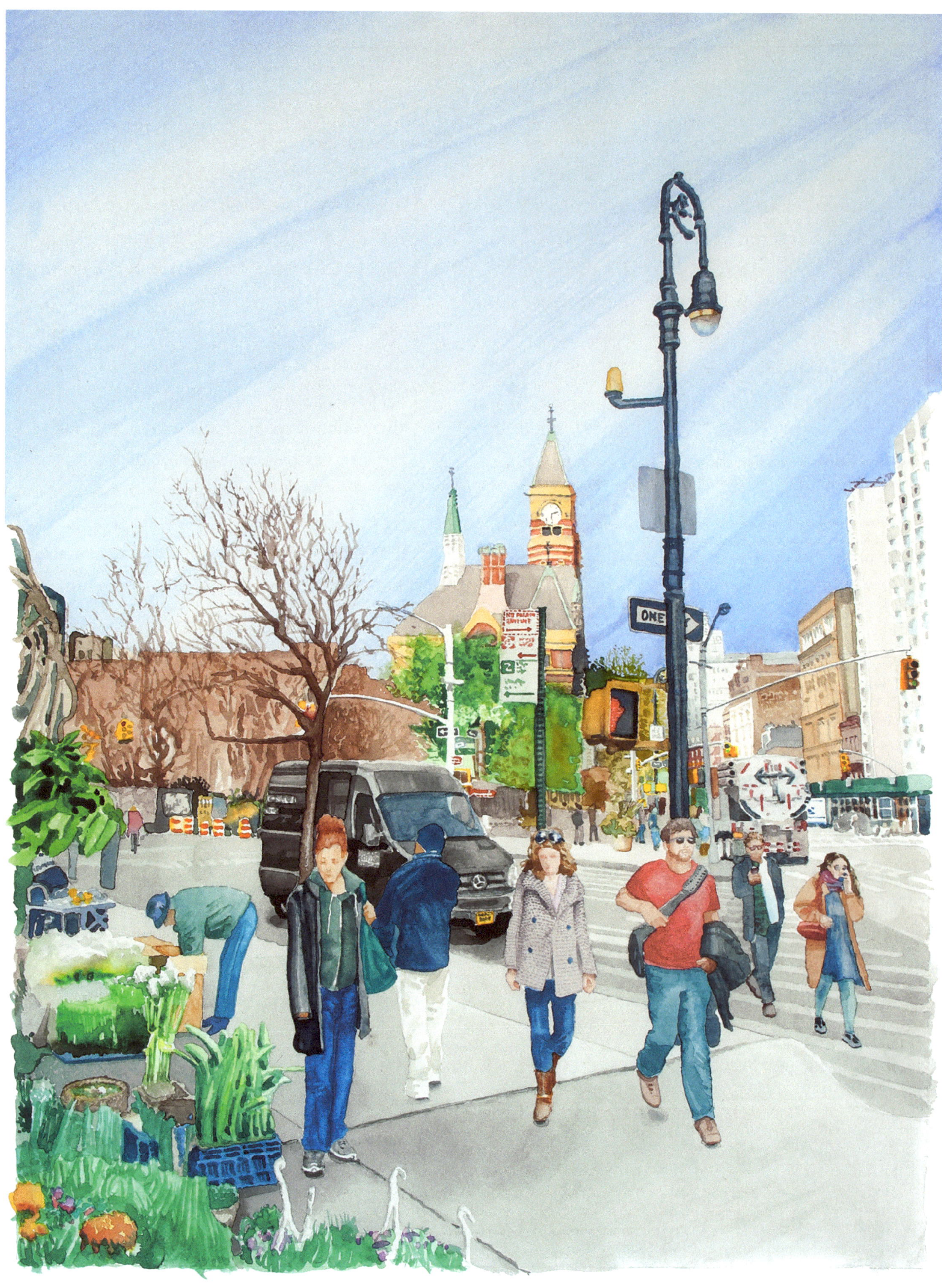
ONE

After winter there is a prespring period in the city which makes you wear a jacket then take it off, then put it back on. I was on a bus once coming in from Caldwell New Jersey and I was sitting next to a woman who had to tell me that her mother insisted on managing the weather with layers. I didn't tell her that you can't argue with your mother and ever win. One of those decisions you make when talking with strangers on a bus. The thing about layers is that they give you great flexibility but you have to carry them around. Freedom but with schlep.

Passing through the seasons reminds us of the past. During one season in my past, I was married, then separated for a few years. I often thought about the years I spent in that relationship, seeing the time as a necessary stage. My anxiety wanted to mark it as a mistake, but a more realistic approach was to see it as a decision I made, that would deftly inform decisions I would make in the future. That first intense relationship was a crucial transition. I would wonder about how she was doing. I got a call recently from her brother to say she had passed away. It was a short, strange call. He offered very little detail. So it goes with what we know and what we will never know. It's the unfinished story and we carry them around like postcards we don't read, hesitant to understand the message. The city keeps moving, gas lines are broken and repaired. I will never know the guy who pulls the wrench, I don't want to, or maybe I do.

If you plant seeds in May, by late July you will have lots of leaves and flowers. I'm thinking of the Impatiens we planted this year. It's amazing! Where did all these pink blossoms come from! Little seeds that looked like mouse poop. OK, if that can happen, everything is so bizarre that the incomprehensible becomes common and the city keeps growing. Our lives keep evolving through it. I often stop, look around, and wonder how the heck all this happened. I'm going to try to put it down, I want to grab the incredible event that is life in the city and wipe it on a piece of paper with approximate color. Then I'm going to look at it and wonder how the heck that happened.

Now we are in the season of the handheld device. It's an uncomfortable theme in my work. I want to include it and show it but I'm not sure it has artistic merit. It is strangely what has happened and the ramifications are unclear at this point. I guess we will have them implanted eventually with some internal interface and that will be even weirder than everyone externally hooked into a device. Of course, only myself and other people who have become old will think it's weird. This is because becoming old is weird.

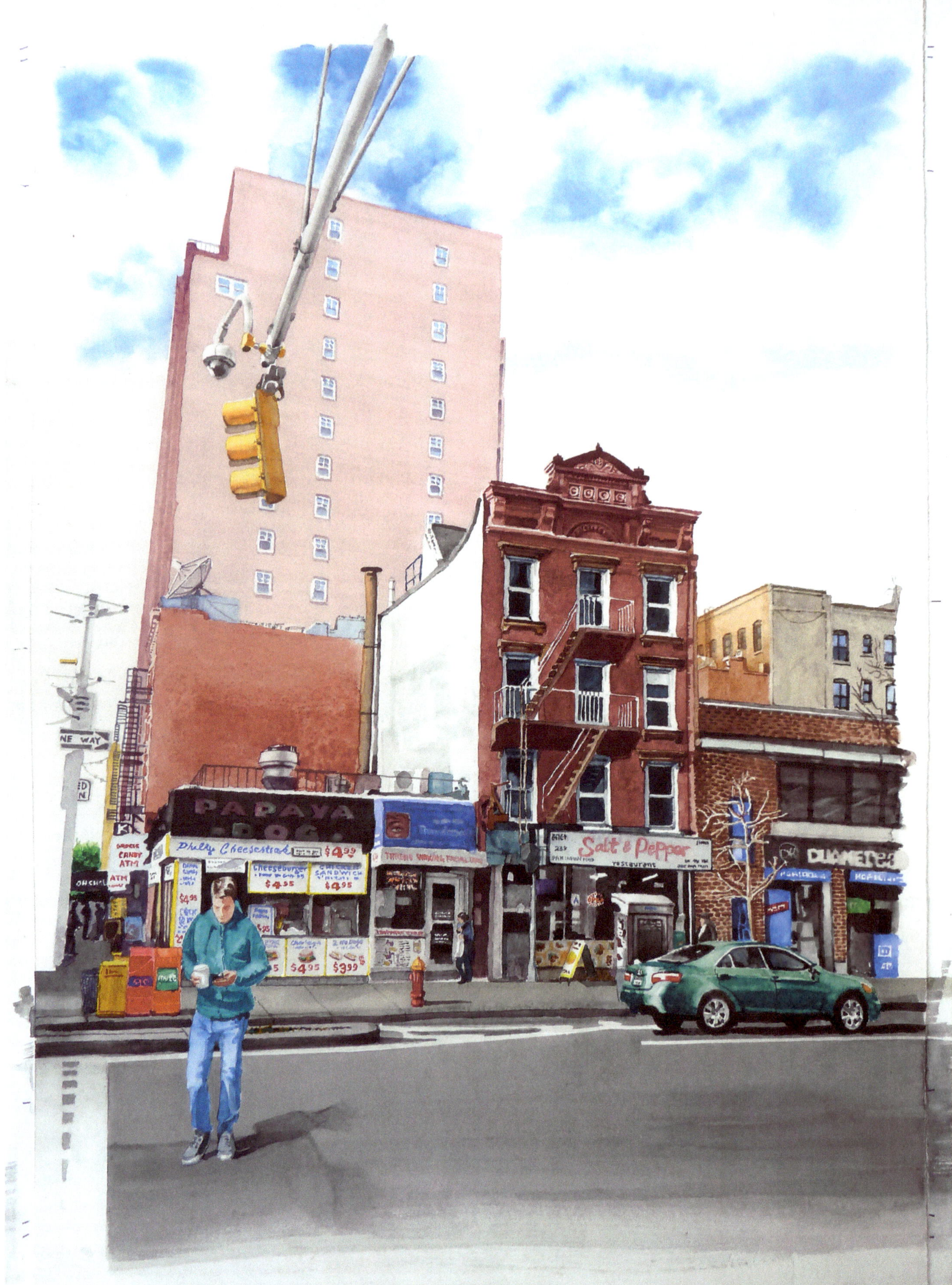
PAPAYA DOG
$4.99
Cheeseburger
SANDWICH
$4.95
$4.95
$3.99
CANDY
ATM
Salt & Pepper
restaurant

14th Street, Second Avenue. Walking across the street with preoccupation is a symbol of the pedestrian culture in the city. Maybe it's a symbol of our current culture. Disregard for the tangible reality surrounding us is a consequence of our current attachment to the virtual reality of immediate but incomplete information.

Immediacy is so appealing, perhaps because life is so short. There really isn't a lot of time to fully live a life and I know this by looking back and wondering why I didn't make better use of years spent drifting along some direction that didn't yield the equivalent value of time spent. Then I get angry with the thought that I have to make every minute count and what about the joy of spare moments? Free mindless strolling about not a care in the world moments? Too many of those and you've lost your life. This fact is in fact debatable, but maybe a balance is required. Part aimless wandering and part incessant, instant access to allegedly everything via technology.

Getting up early, really early, and running into the living room to turn on cartoons was a concept that invariably produced joy in the heart of a young me. Now the thought of getting up really early produces anxiety and stress. Not really. I get up early sometimes, no problem. The idea of charging out into the world for new conquest still inspires a young innocent surge of intrepid adventure. This is the lure of the city and the treasures therein. One has to be satisfied with treasure as hot dogs or toothpaste, but with a little extra effort, more valuable bounty is at hand.

A strictly visual treat is sometimes enough. A juxtaposition of old and new is always alluring because it places the passage of time into one moment of gazing. I get to contrast the fossilized remains with a recently manufactured footprint and everything in between. My eyes are old but my glasses are new and I can see. This is how all the days of achievement and floundering make sense. It's crossing the street that you always cross and feeling like it might be a new street and the old one as well. You can see your past footprints as you make new ones.

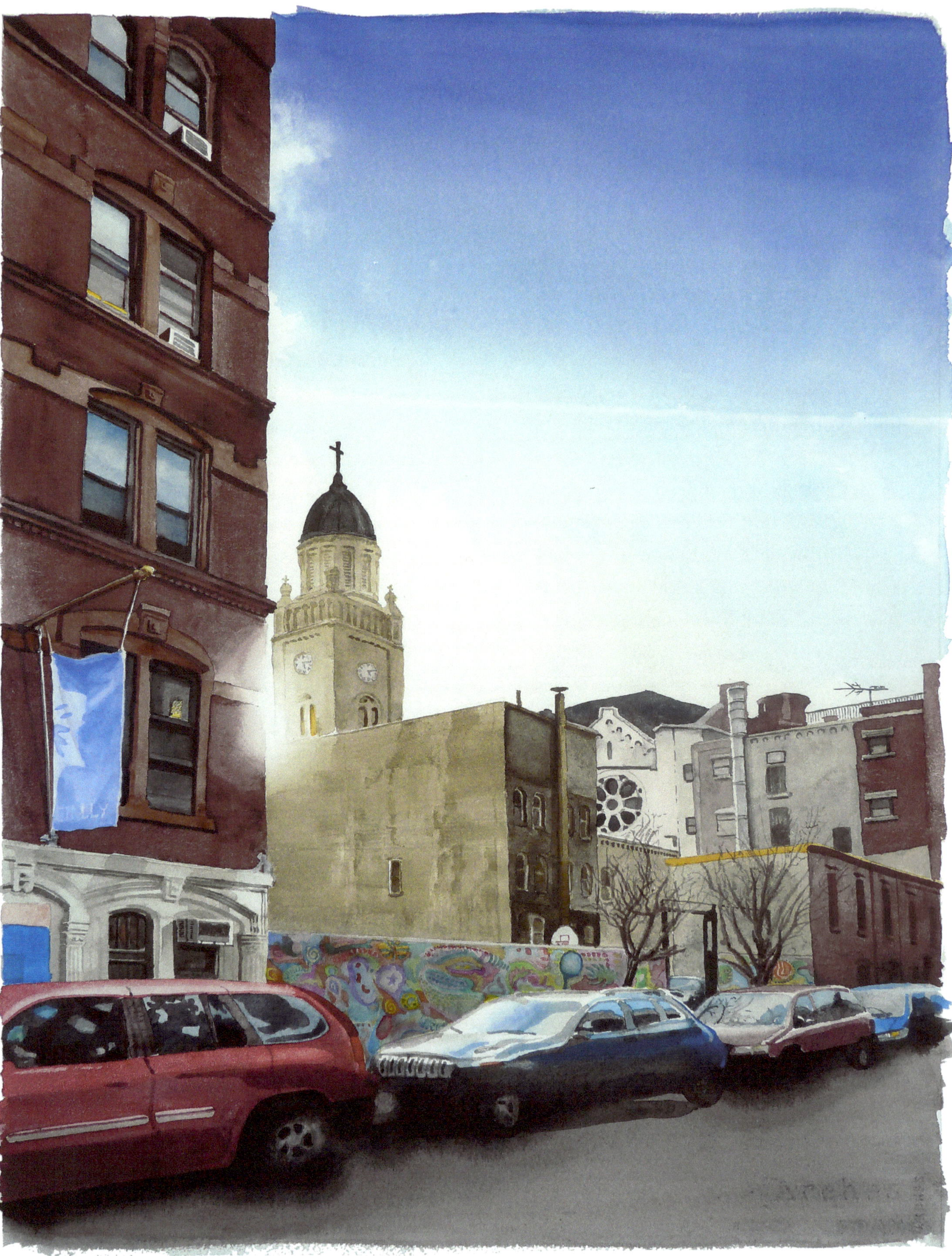

I was walking west on 4th Street just off Avenue B, late afternoon, pondering the jet stream chalk strokes that are as common as clouds. They are temporary marks of passage, kind of like all the sidewalks I have been walking on. There are more permanent marks on the wall of a schoolyard, and a banner that will probably be different on my next fly by. Car windows are usually looked out of and now they are looking out at me. They are looking at me with distorted versions of the immediate surroundings. I'm thinking it's like the news. Reporting back what's happening all around but warped by curvature and tint. This is how I listen to the news, as an unreliable report regarding true actuality but derivative.

My paintings are derivative car window reflections of the city. I try to minimize the distortion. People who write about art use the word interpretation and it is a kind of personal unavoidable distortion. I frequently torture the woman in my life by recounting stories she has heard over and over. She stops me after the first two or at most three words and says "Oh yeah, this is the one where..." Her recollection is mostly accurate but the detail is always embellished or abbreviated according to her version. Often it's a condensed news headline and serves to save her from reiterating the frayed details again. My interpretation or distortion of the glimpse I take from the city is a report stated in my visual language which I hope is multi-lingual.

Using a visual language is the way to talk to people of all languages but it is open to infinite variations of interpretation. This is acceptable because I'm not going for the actuality as much as the feeling and that can translate into a personal experience which is why I do this to begin with. I want to provide an experience that is so personal that no one other than the beholder can put it into truly accurate words for themselves. This is of course ironic because I'm using all these words. If you like the pictures don't worry about the words. It's not about the words ultimately but you might like the words, so they are here if you want them.

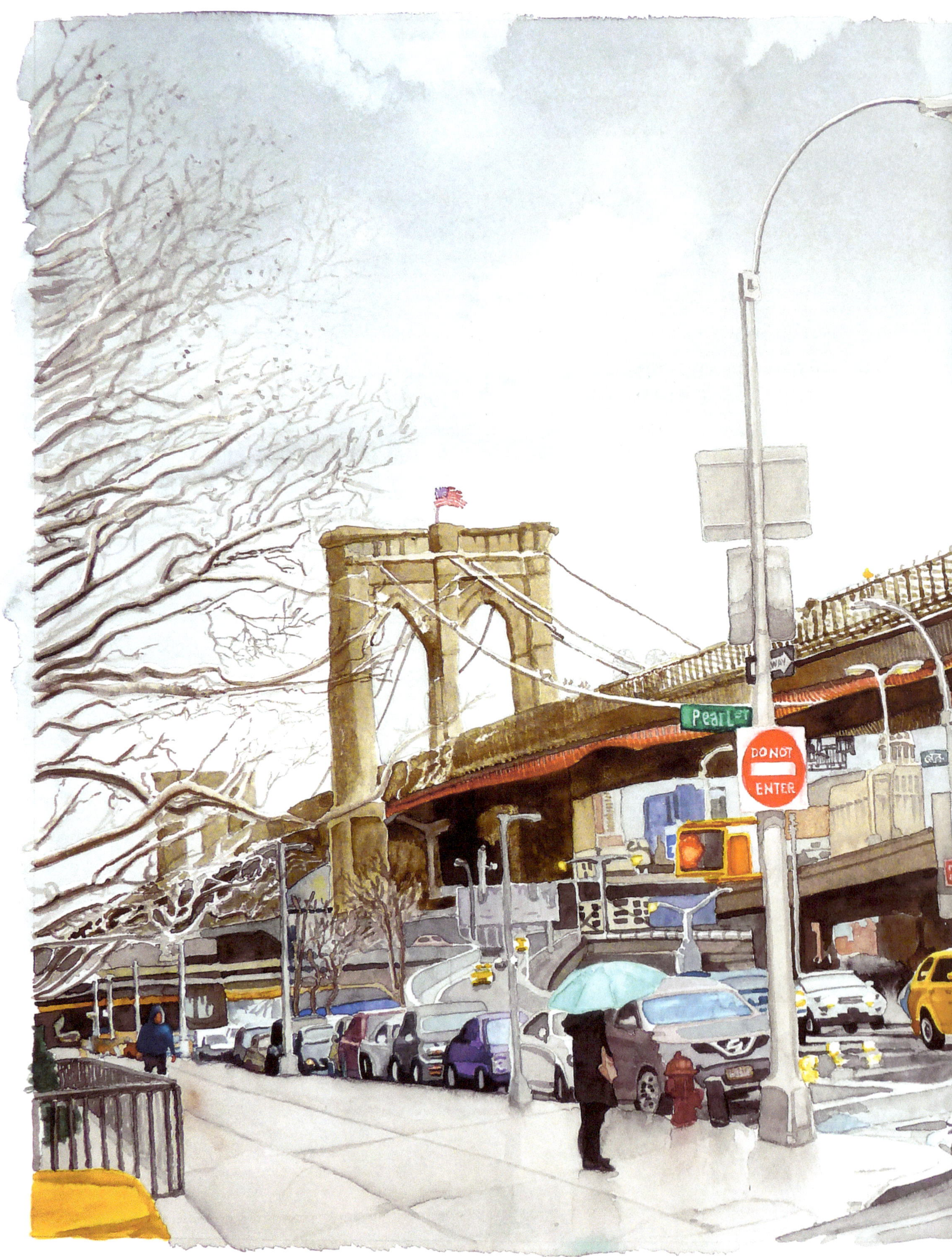

WAY
Pearl St
DO NOT
ENTER

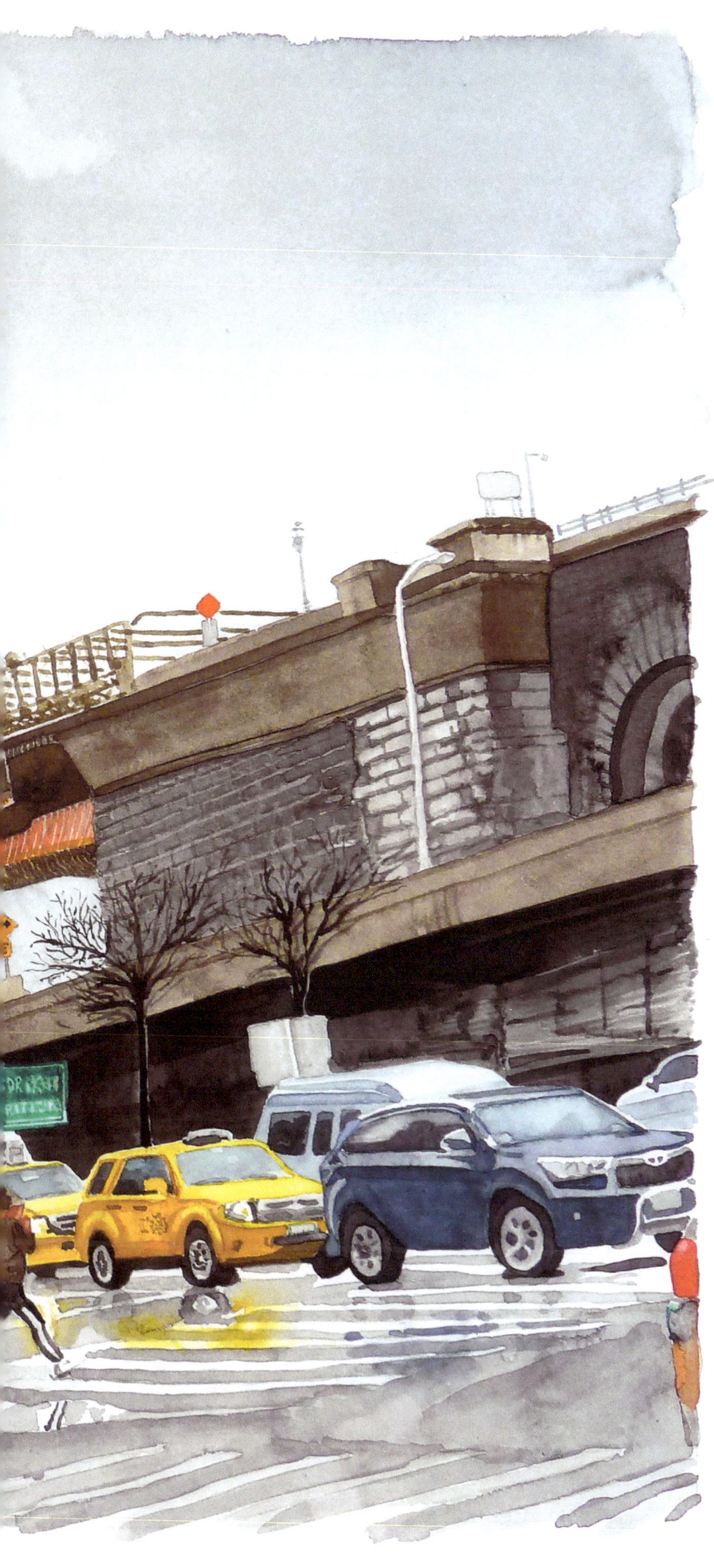

Going to work early in the morning in the rain. The feeling I get from this routine is somewhat negative and tinged with dread. An exacerbated version of having to get out of bed and not wanting to or even worse than that. The traffic is a slippery, cold, impatient swarm activity. Any talk about living life stress-free, being calm, balanced and thoughtful, is nice work if you can get it, mostly it's a luxury only someone who doesn't have to work gets to enjoy. Not being tied to making money is perfect when you don't need to make money. Others get to work.

I'm sure this bridge was built on days like this, cold hands and feet putting bricks on bricks, then more bricks. Commuting, tasking, fulfilling someone else's expectations, are like laying bricks that you hope will become something that you built. The pain is tolerable if you know you are building a bridge. It's safe passage to where you want to be eventually. Make sure you are building a bridge.

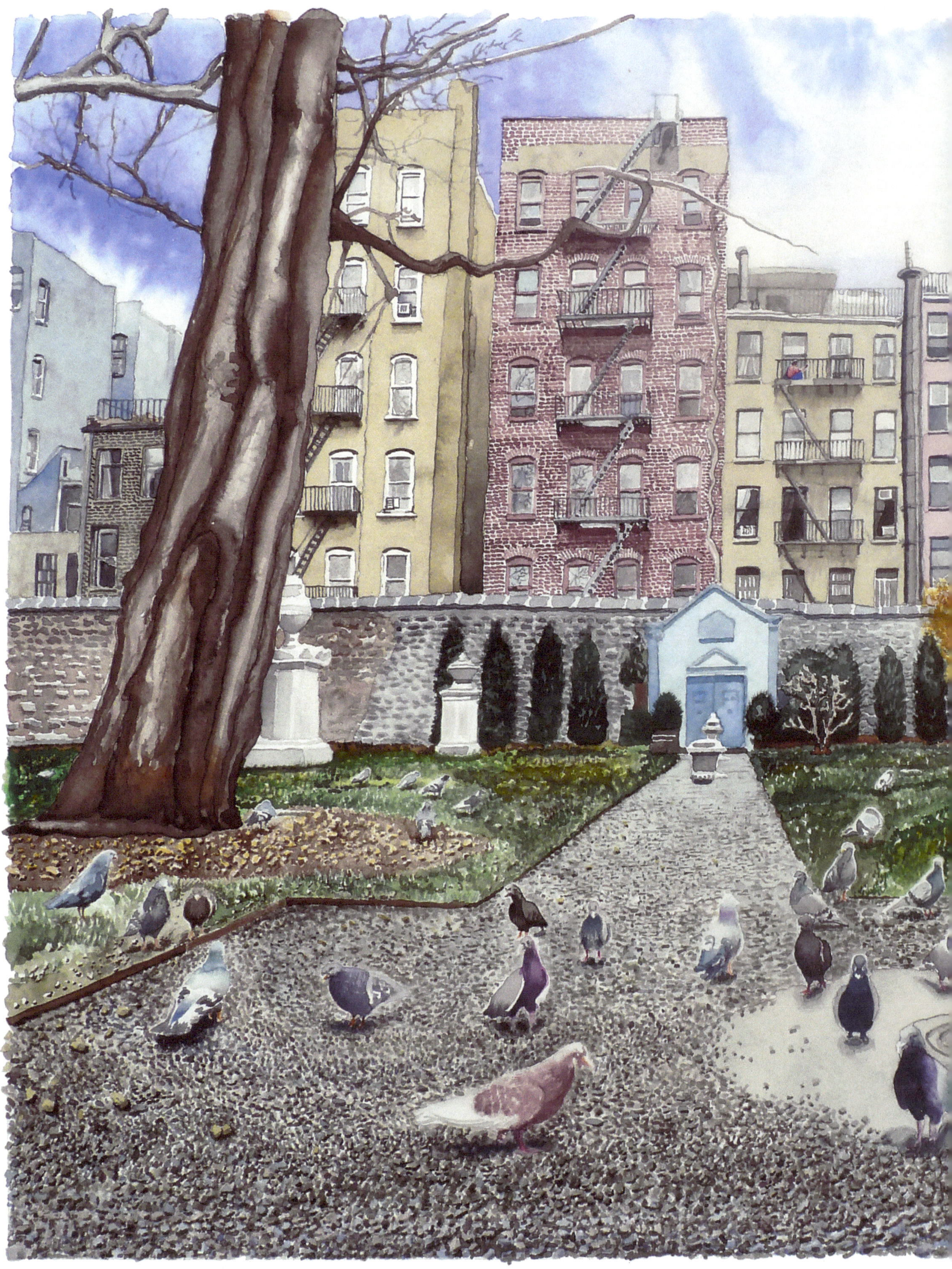

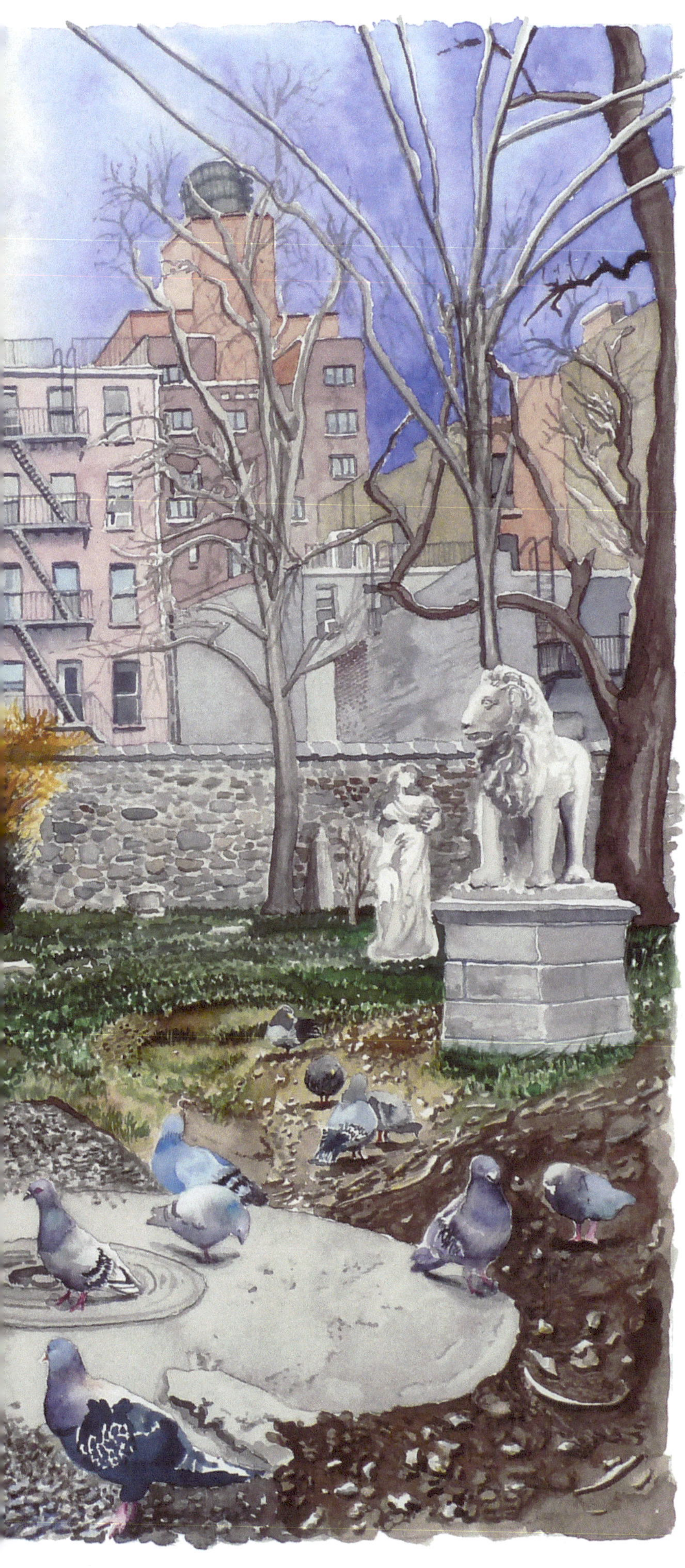

I had an accountant once who tried to talk me out of buying a life insurance policy, to benefit and protect the woman in my life, whom I cherish more than breath, in the event of my untimely death. He said, and I'm not kidding, "Why do you care? You'll be dead!"

Cemeteries are few but evident in the city and the one on 11th Street is serene and somewhat of a pigeon hangout. I'm sure that the deceased folks there are no one I have ever known, perhaps I would know of them.

When I walk past a cemetery in the city I always stop and look and think fondly of the folks who lived in whatever bliss and turmoil they had as part of a lifetime. They have left me this idea that once they were here, in a place probably quite different than it is now.

If the guy on the fire escape stops looking at his phone and looks over here at the statues and the pigeons he might get a chance to think about his short life and where he might end up, and what that might be about.

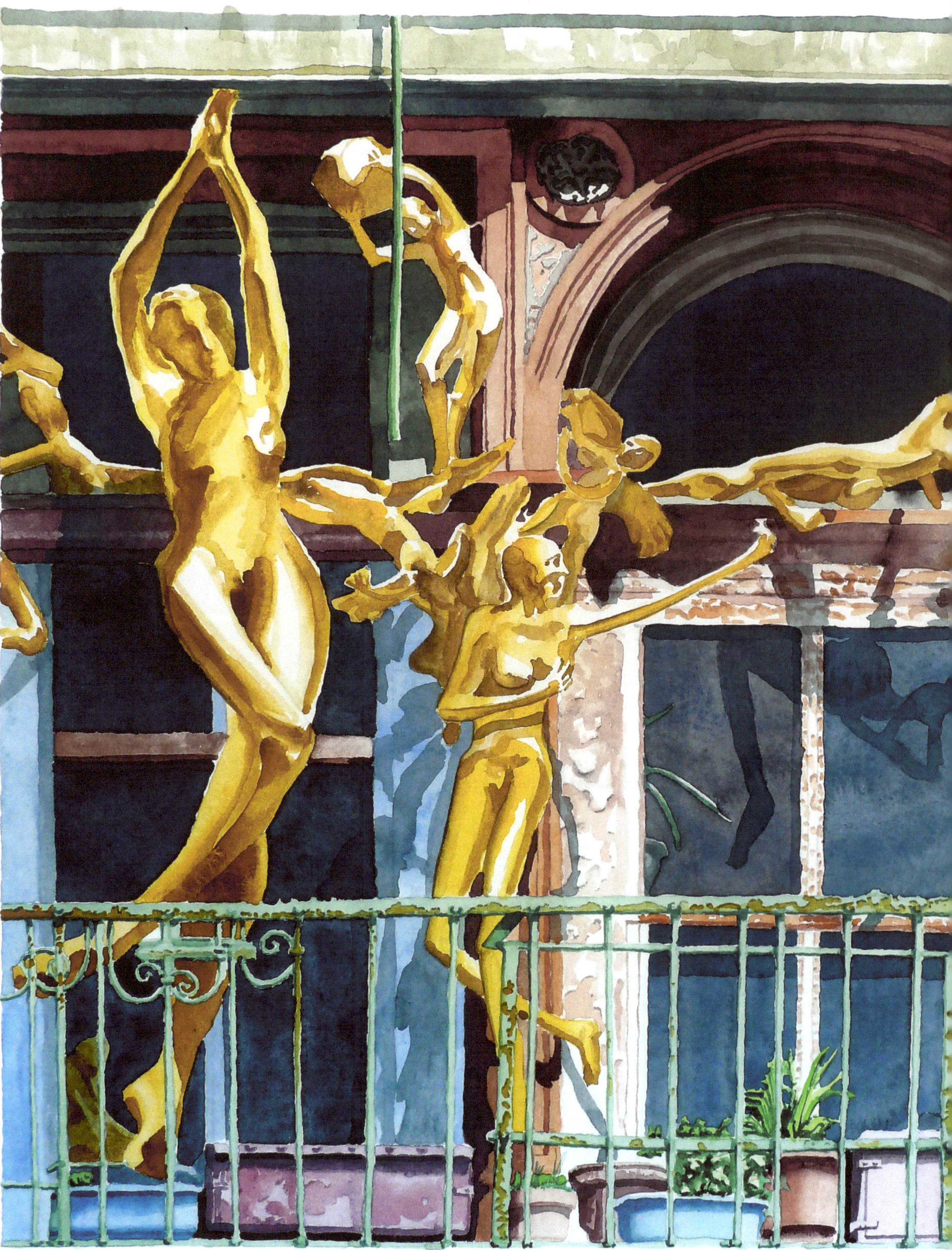

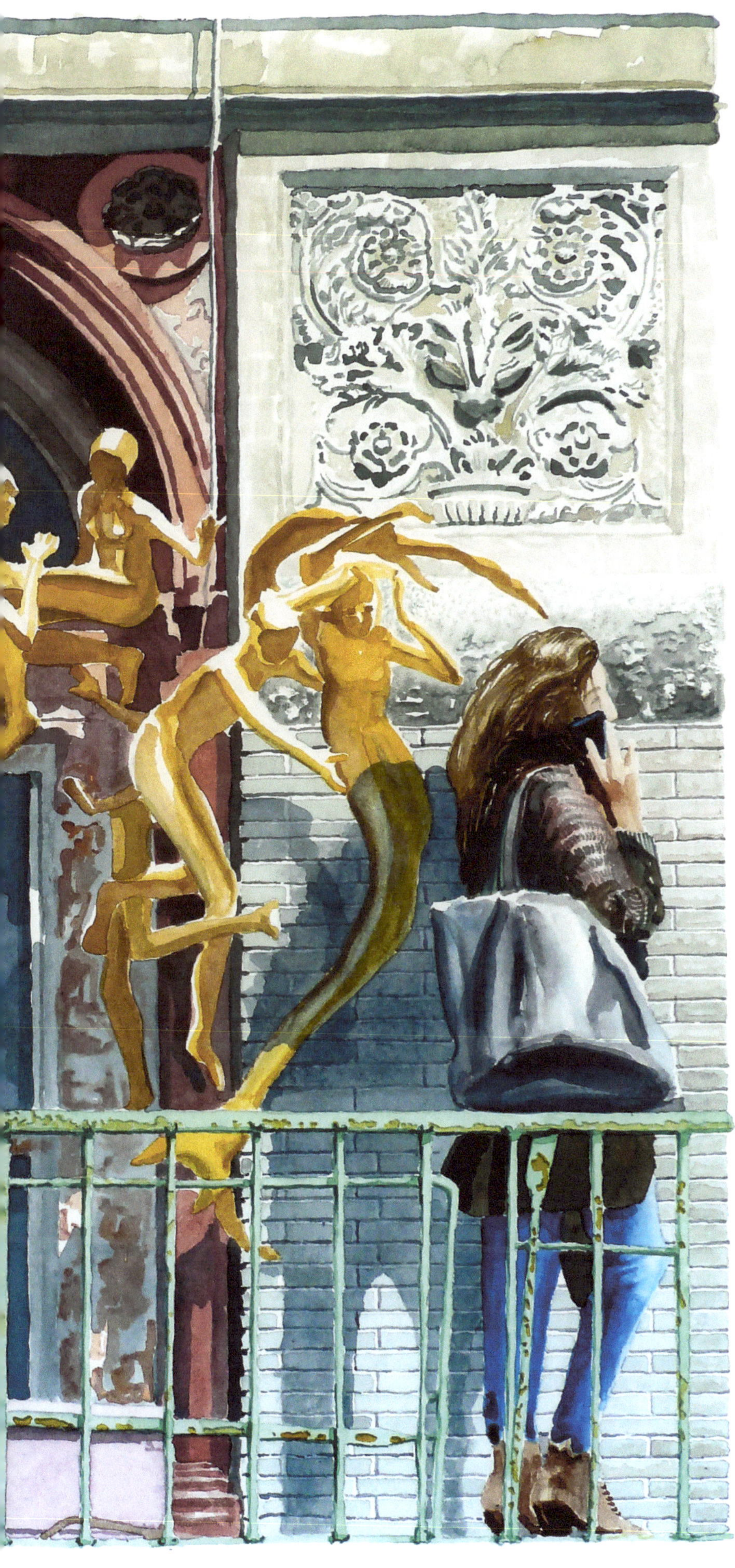

Walking through the embellished streets and avenues of the city will saturate you with detail. You have to look and absorb the uniqueness, the unexpected. Bond Street for instance, just off Broadway, will give you a glimpse of the esoteric. There are gold figures attached to the side of a building and they are perched with the authority of an artistic endeavor made some time ago. They are part of a wildly creative urban tapestry. I noticed a young lady on a balcony near these statues, oblivious to their beckoning mystery. She was preoccupied with her handheld device, as is the case today everywhere I turn. I'm sure she was engaged in a mission-critical communication and the gold figures understood this and were emulating her intense concentration with mystical gestures of concern. I hope her vital communications were received with the urgency and importance intended.

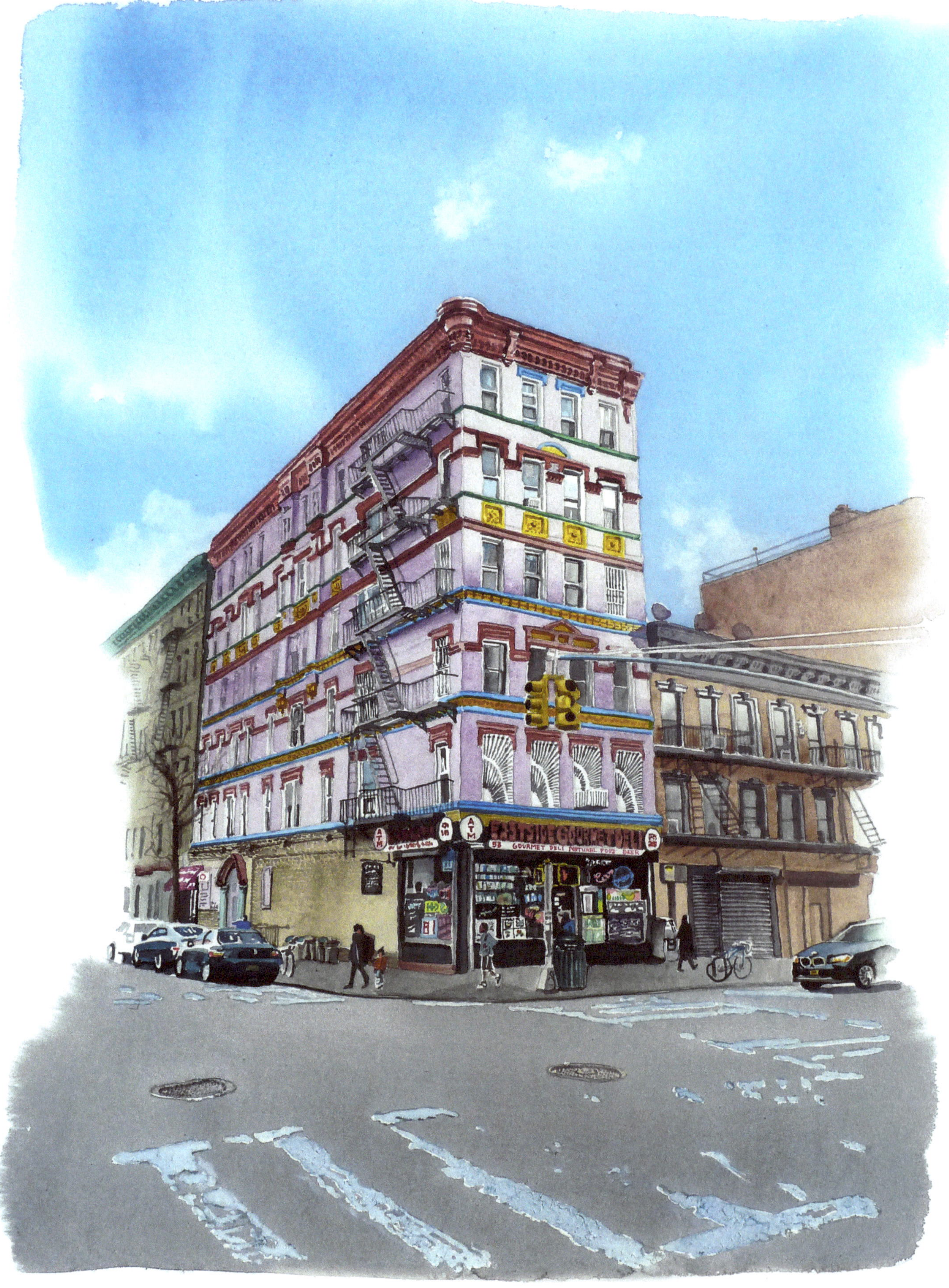
ATM
ATM
EAST SIDE GOURMET DELI
53 GOURMET DELI NATURAL FOOD BEER

Avenue B and Fourth Street. The lavender building that stands as a shout of color and punctuation on the corner confirmed my experience of being astounded in this city of the astounding. The hum and churn of motion surrounding one's passage through the forest of buildings are often piqued by an exclamation point. This dilute plum, gold, russet sentinel attests to the uniqueness and bold expression of the Lower East Side.

I used to live on Avenue B and Third Street, back in 1979. There was much less color then. Ambition and hope were my colors, naive enthusiasm in your pallet works wonders when painting a future.

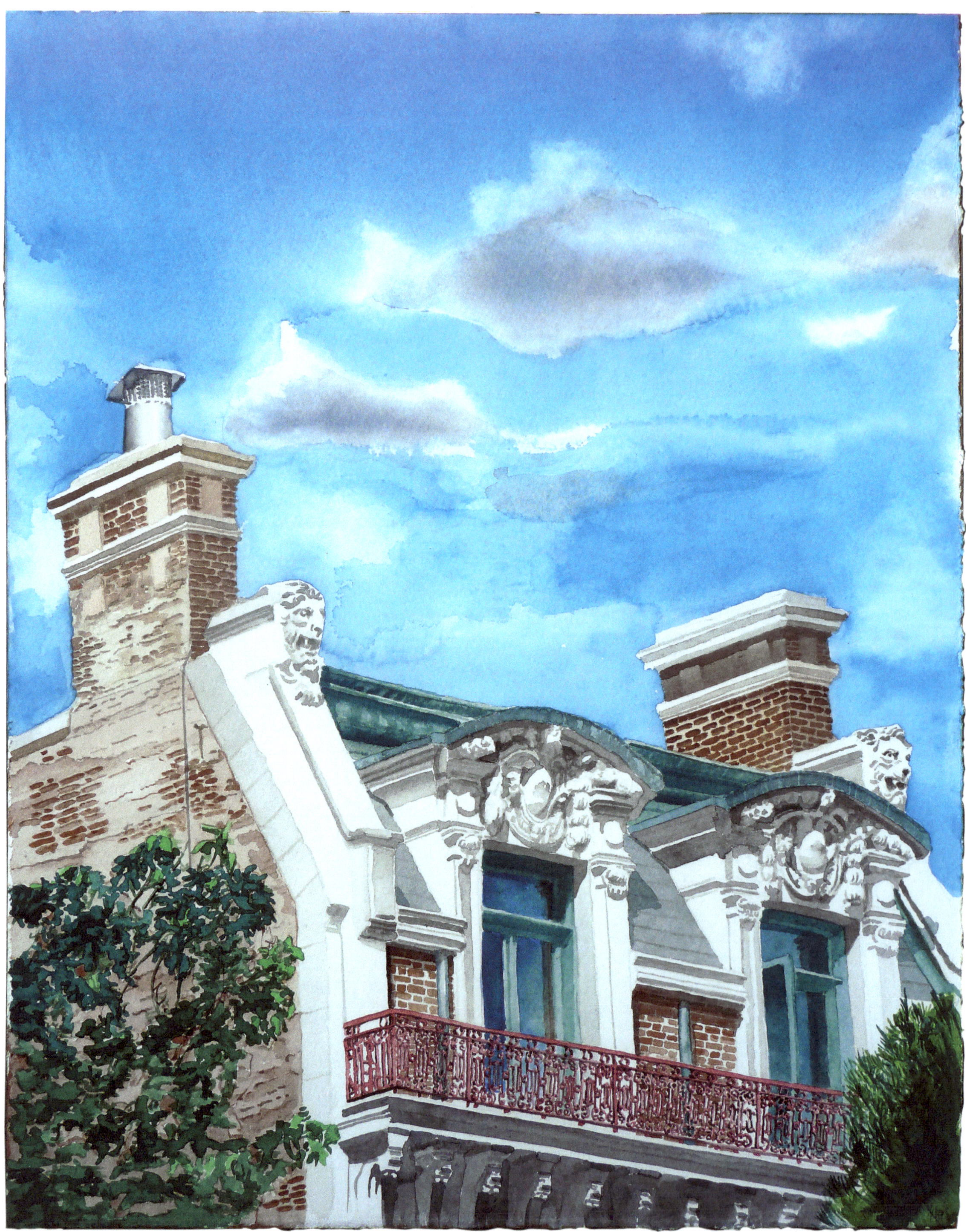

Who was it who once walked out onto a wrought iron balcony beneath this Gothic detail? Who was it, who looked out with a distracted air of entitlement? I assume many have over the years and I don't believe they had the perspective that I have. I don't think we would have shared a proletariat point of view, more likely they would have fostered the mindset of the old world aristocracy.

Regardless of the random allocation of social status at birth, purely as a pedestrian individual looking up from the sidewalk, I behold these impressive facades with reverence. I relate to the artists, architects, masons and the skills that it took to create a structure that could only be found in a great city or a storybook. The trees support this superb image in their untiring quest for sunlight. This precious light streams onto all surfaces with a complete lack of discretion, thankfully.

Rich dwelling space, elegant space, interiors robust with refinement, share a close proximity with those around the corner sleeping on the sidewalk. The disparity is stunning. I chafe against this huge margin of fortune and the evident broad range and scale of prosperity. I have landed somewhere on the curve as everyone does, part luck, part work, part tenacity. The concept of deservedness is inapplicable. Yet there it is, the beauty, the majesty, and the misfortune, dotting the city scene with indiscriminate pointillism. We live amongst it, we live with it.

I was not born into a world where lofty opportunities rising from a fertile bed of wealth surrounded my future. I have never slept on a sidewalk. I earn my daily bread, and I appreciate this city by painting it, from my vantage point. The point where I look up and see the beauty.

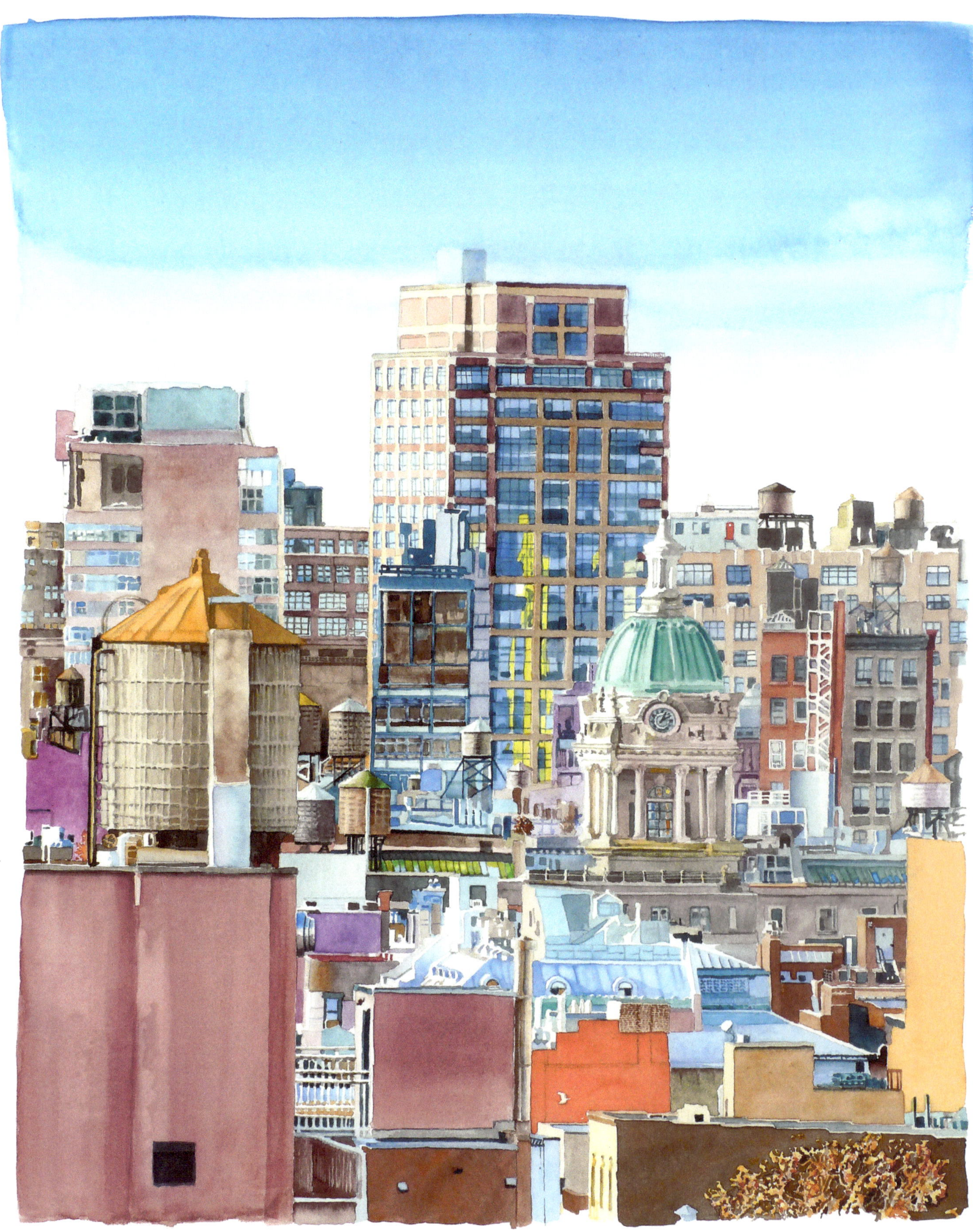

The sprawl. Looking out from the modest terrace of our apartment on the 16th floor of a building on Grand Street facing west. This is in the direction of Soho, Tribeca, some of downtown, uptown and the complexity of old and new that exist there. Each window foretells a story and a segment of life in time. Commerce, business, leisure, sleep, laughter, heated arguments and nothing at all are all going on in simultaneous cacophony. Each building has a purpose and each is in the process of construction and decay. Iconic water towers, provide water pressure and fire protection for buildings more than six stories. Light travels through glass into rooms where unknown activities transpire, or if no one is there, it's a quiet nascent tableau.

The rooftops are places to escape to, either designed for that purpose or strictly utility in nature. Often when gazing across this densely assorted tundra, people can be seen pacing about in a moment of respite from otherwise purposeful activities. Standing aside from the experience of stress, having rare time to think about things there is never time to think of, is the luxury of an escape to the rooftop. You can look outside or inside yourself. You can look around, and not commit to thinking anything, which is difficult but for me at least, rewarding. Looking at windows is a challenge not to compare what you see as something better than what you have. What you see will be a limited hint and the seduction is to imagine how much better that must be than where you are. There will be someone out there looking out the window seeing you on the rooftop and thinking the same thing. What kind of freedom lies behind that luxury tinted glass really, but perhaps it's better there after all, no matter, you are here taking it in within at least a minute of reflection.

The green dome of the old police station, now luxury lofts for fashion models, celebrities and wealth managers, stands out like a gemstone among other stones in a riverbed. The clock looking out is an icon on Centre Street, it tells us what's important and what isn't. What things were, what they are, and to some degree what they will become. Change is constant yet some things will remain, how they have been, somewhat changed, holding the old image of themselves up in a crowd of mostly indifferent faces. I say mostly because I am in that crowd, I am far from indifferent, yet I remain just a fragment, a single face.

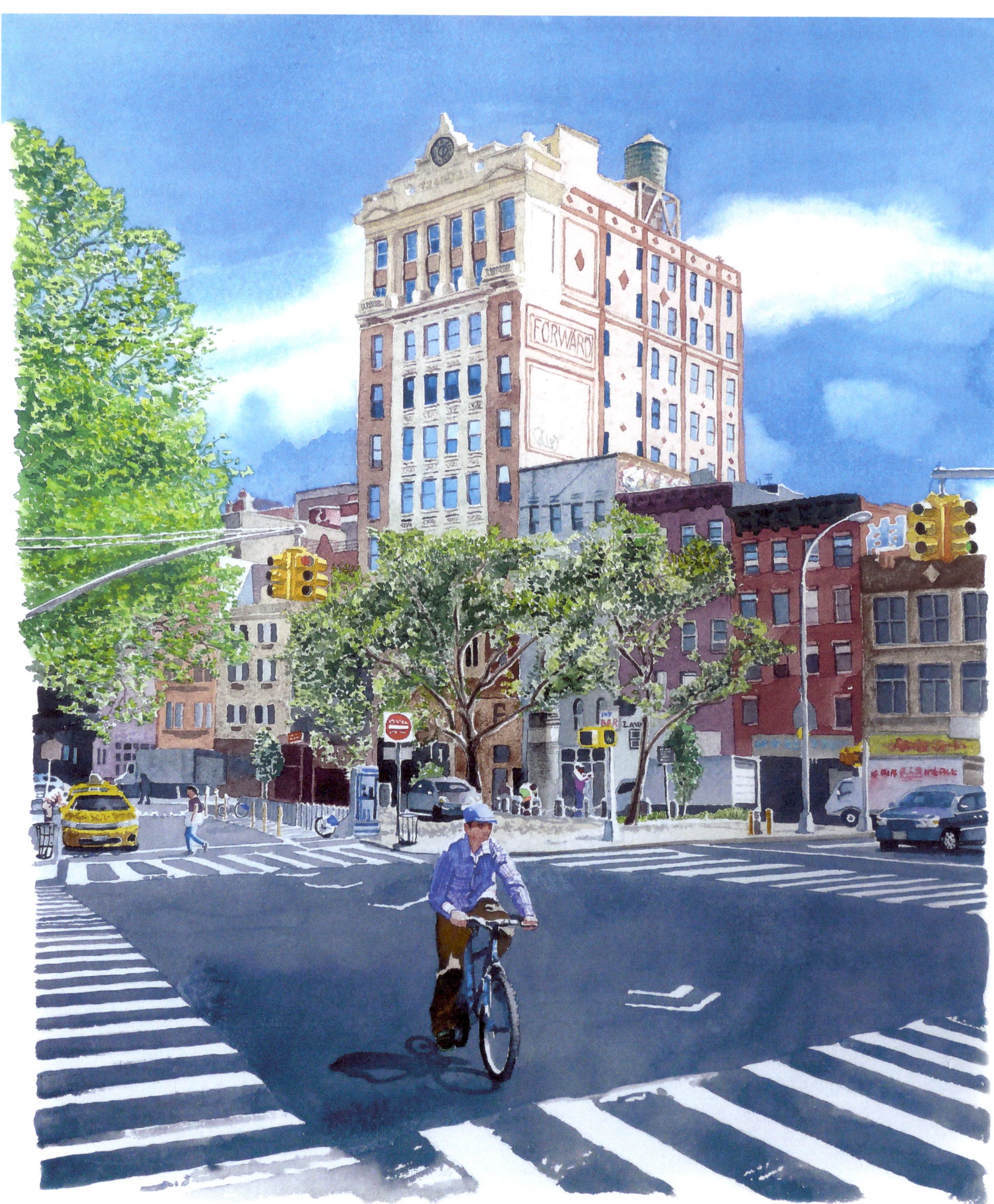
FORWARD

The lower east side, Grand Street, East Broadway, Rutgers, are places like all the cloistered nooks in the city, uniquely their own universe. The Forward building, once the headquarters for a Yiddish Socialist newspaper, now luxury condos, has traded social service for status living but the majesty of its profile in the neighborhood remains. People still walk about on their way to making a life with the same steps on the street. Vital tasks or casual exploration pedal past through the intersection of Rutgers and Canal. Islands between streets are vantage points to get bearings, to decide how to go.

I used to make very rare deliveries to this part of town when I rode a bike for a living and it was always a trip to the other side of the tracks. Even earlier, when all I knew how to do was work behind a counter only a year after coming here by myself, I worked at a diner called Aldo's, on Grand Street. Every morning I put a red rimmed white porcelain cup on a saucer, poured black coffee to the brim and ceremoniously set it before an old guy named Mike. Mike came to Aldo's every day at 9:00 am. He wore a paper napkin folded around his wrist under his watch band. His coffee would spill a little and I would give him a napkin to put on the saucer. He would say "That's right, everything easy." Mike had lived here for forty years and he liked to have his coffee at Aldo's. He would say, "Aldo, you still here?" Aldo, who sat in the far corner tucked behind a Formica and chrome rimmed tabletop would say "Yea Mike. You OK?" Mike would say "Oh yea. Everything easy." Every morning.

The thing about Mike's assessment for how things should be, everything, I'm thinking comes from a lifetime of everything hard. Hard to be accepted for who you really are, hard to keep your skills relevant, hard to keep making a living, year after year. Hard to get along with everyone, your wife, the guy who pays you to do something. Hard to compete. Hard to be flexible, to love something, or not to hate everything. I'm thinking it was really hard for Mike, and now he wants it to be easy. Easy is good, easy is a relief.

After my shift, I would walk to the subway with Manny the cook. He would take dice from his pocket and roll them on the sidewalk while we were walking in a hurry, the result would determine to ride on the D train or the F train to his wife and kids somewhere in Brooklyn. I would take the D uptown to Columbus circle, to 63rd Street, to the Y.

Living here is sometimes a gamble. You make decisions based on how much you choose to risk. Some take no risks, and some take too many. I look back on the dice I threw to get wherever I am now and maybe I should have rolled better. You can always say that. I rolled and now I'm here, and I will roll again.

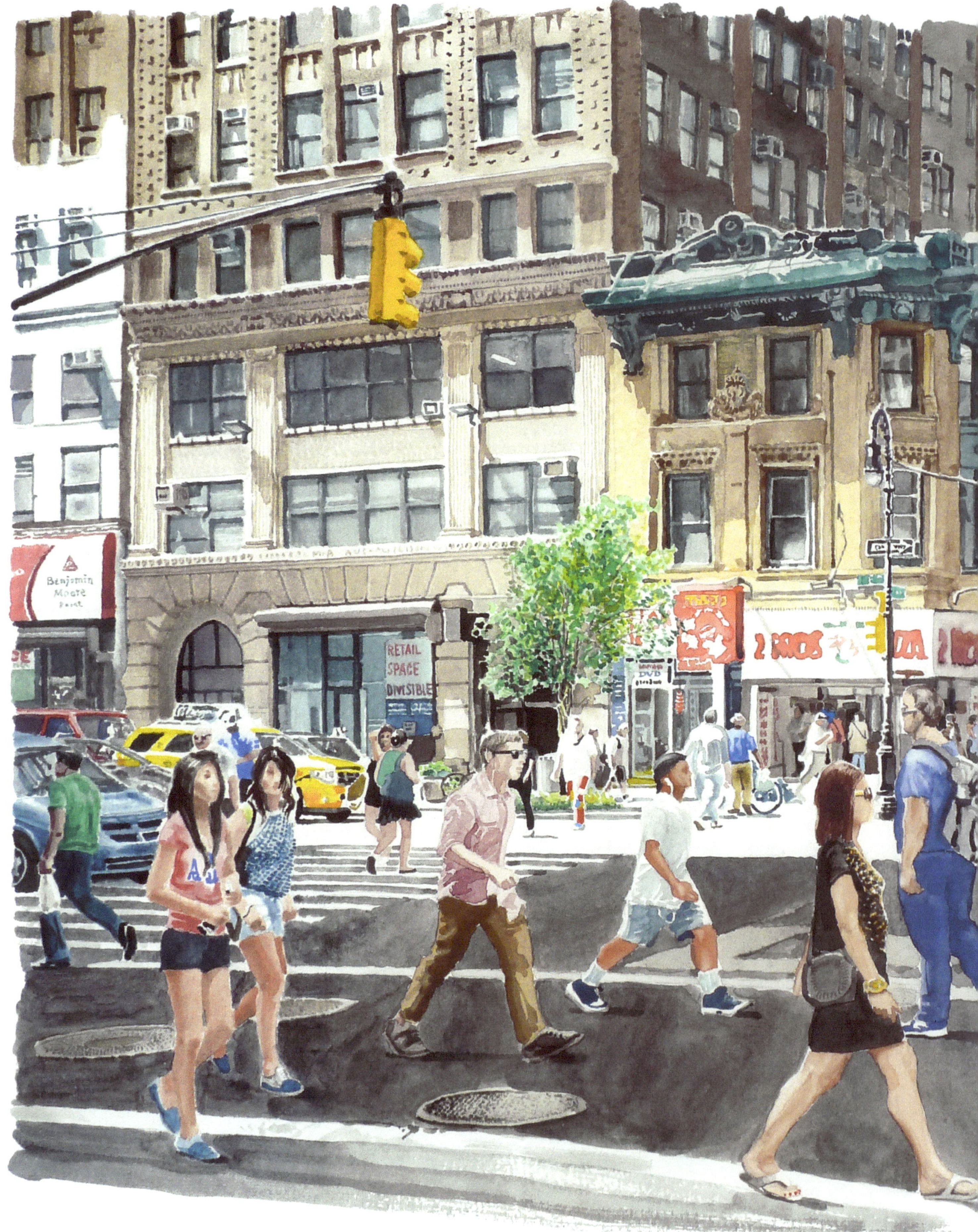
Benjamin Moore Paint
RETAIL SPACE DIVISIBLE
DVD

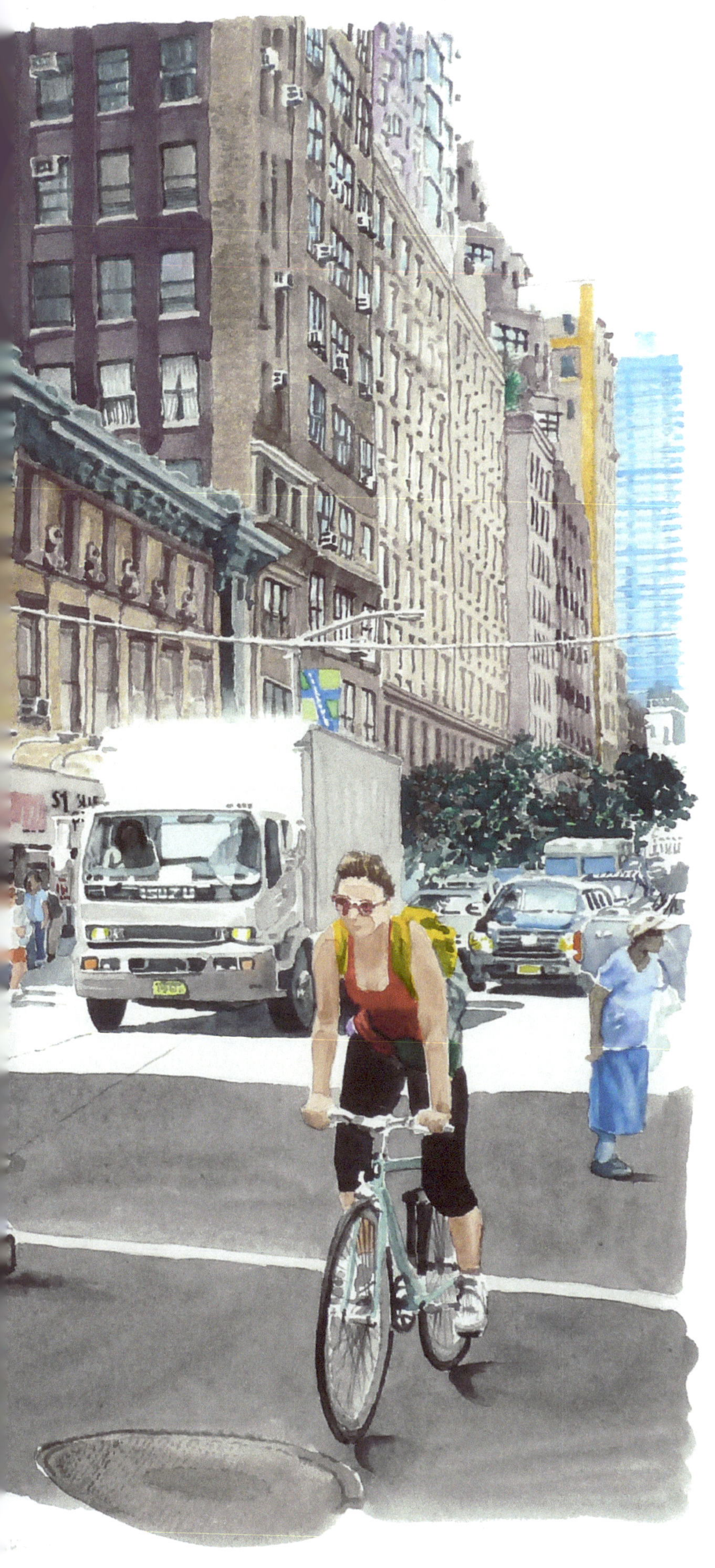

44th Street and Eighth Avenue at lunchtime on a sunny day in late summer is where you will see multiple inner dialogues going on simultaneously. How many are specific to the individual and how many are general and common. Some of it is pure utility and maybe the street is a place to be free from your normal narrative. Walking is enough of a mild distraction to take the mind off of concentrated preoccupation, so for me, it lets my thoughts have permission to fly around and express freely. A busy sidewalk has enough raw material to fuel launching into thought patterns you might not be inspired by otherwise. Sometimes I find myself being angry about something. Am I picking up the feeling of defensive angst around me? Am I absorbing the surplus of road rage knocking off the walls of buildings? Then the buildings might have inner thoughts as well, not just the myriad souls coming in and out, but thoughts about how they were built, and what they have become. How the traffic of souls has changed, who are the occupants now, who did they used to be. If I were a building, I might be stoic and removed from feeling, having endured weather and the constant abrasion of habitation and re-habitation. I would be defensive because inadequacy of construction or design created my condition and it wasn't my fault. Shouting out to the occupants, I might say this is who I am, it wasn't my idea, I just am this way. There are better buildings and worse, far worse, and I am only this and when I am over I will fall away into the earth.

For now I am this building at this moment. Bricks, windows, wrought iron, plaster, old flakes of paint, a basement boiler, stairs, doors, hallways with one small window at the end by the stairwell. Rooms for living, rooms for doing business, rooms for keeping things safe, a room to hold the machine that runs the elevator.

In the building that is myself, there are rooms I am in and out of all the time. Rooms where I see people, rooms I visit infrequently, rooms I never go into. Rooms that have stuff in them I don't want to see. Rooms of stuff I should get rid of. Rooms that are packed with things that I want to look over when I'm ready. Rooms I have never entered, as well as rooms I never intend to enter, but probably should. After all, the rooms are here, they are part of my building. I am both afraid and challenged, it's my building that I built but there are things I did to build it that I regret. I might want to go back and look at what is really there.

Why invite re-experiencing trauma? My father never talked about being in a prisoner of war camp. Never said one word about it to me. If I asked, he would get mad. There were rooms in his building that were locked. Now mine are as well, and I know how I got here, so maybe I understand him better.

When I worked for a design firm, I used to have these long philosophical talks with the creative director in his office when the day was done and things had cleared out a bit. He was also the owner, the name of the company was his name. Once when I was telling him about a serious unresolvable life situation I had stumbled onto over the years, he said that sometimes you have to put things into a box, and close the lid. The thing works the lid open and comes out periodically and you have to gently push it back in and close the lid again. I accused him of avoidance behavior and denial, and he said, "This might be something you can't fix or even get real closure on and you have to put it away. It will always be there. You allow for it, it's your thing, but it belongs in the box."

So I'm looking out the window of my building, I'm OK, I'm safe, and there are many rooms, and I'm looking out of the one I'm in right now.

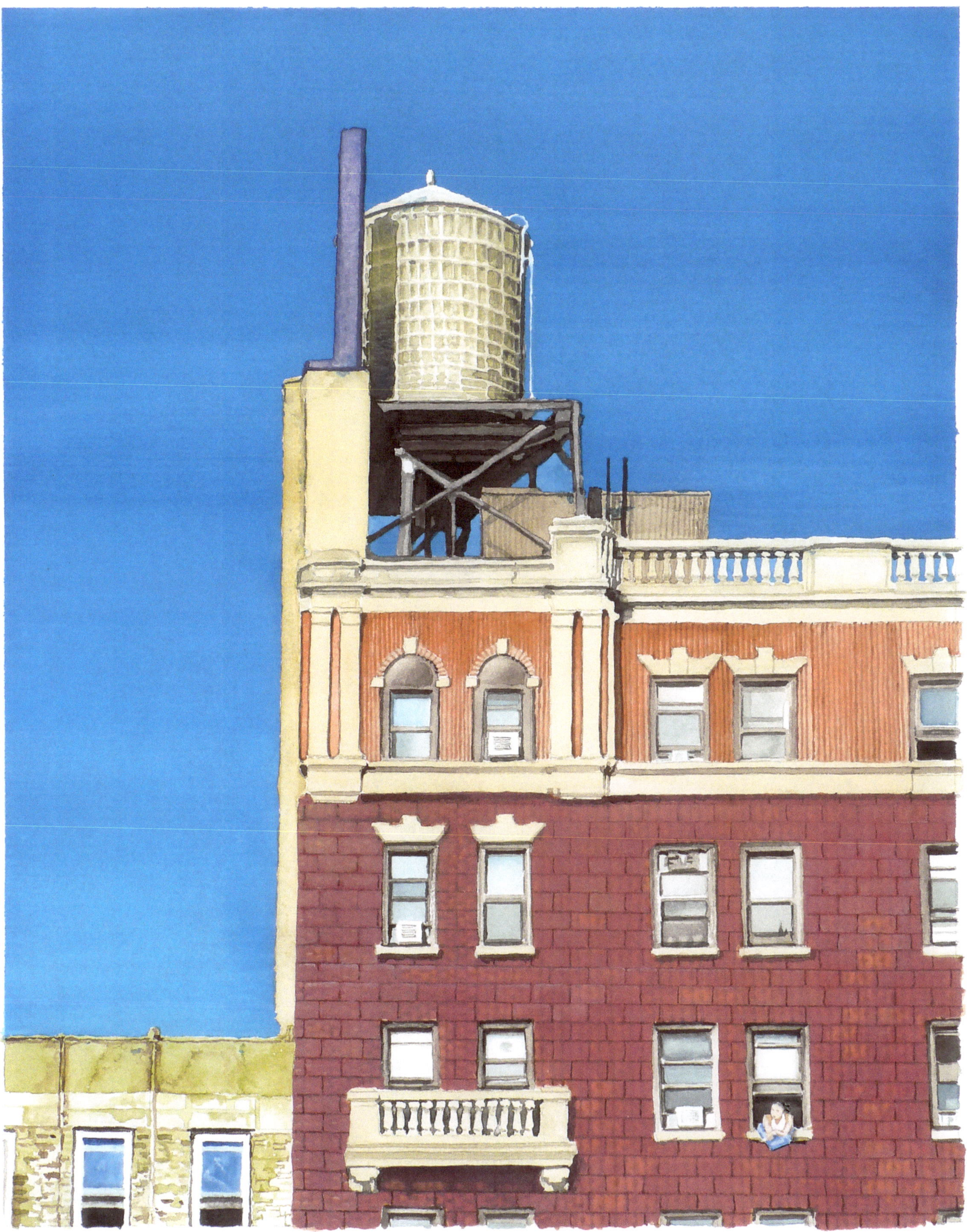

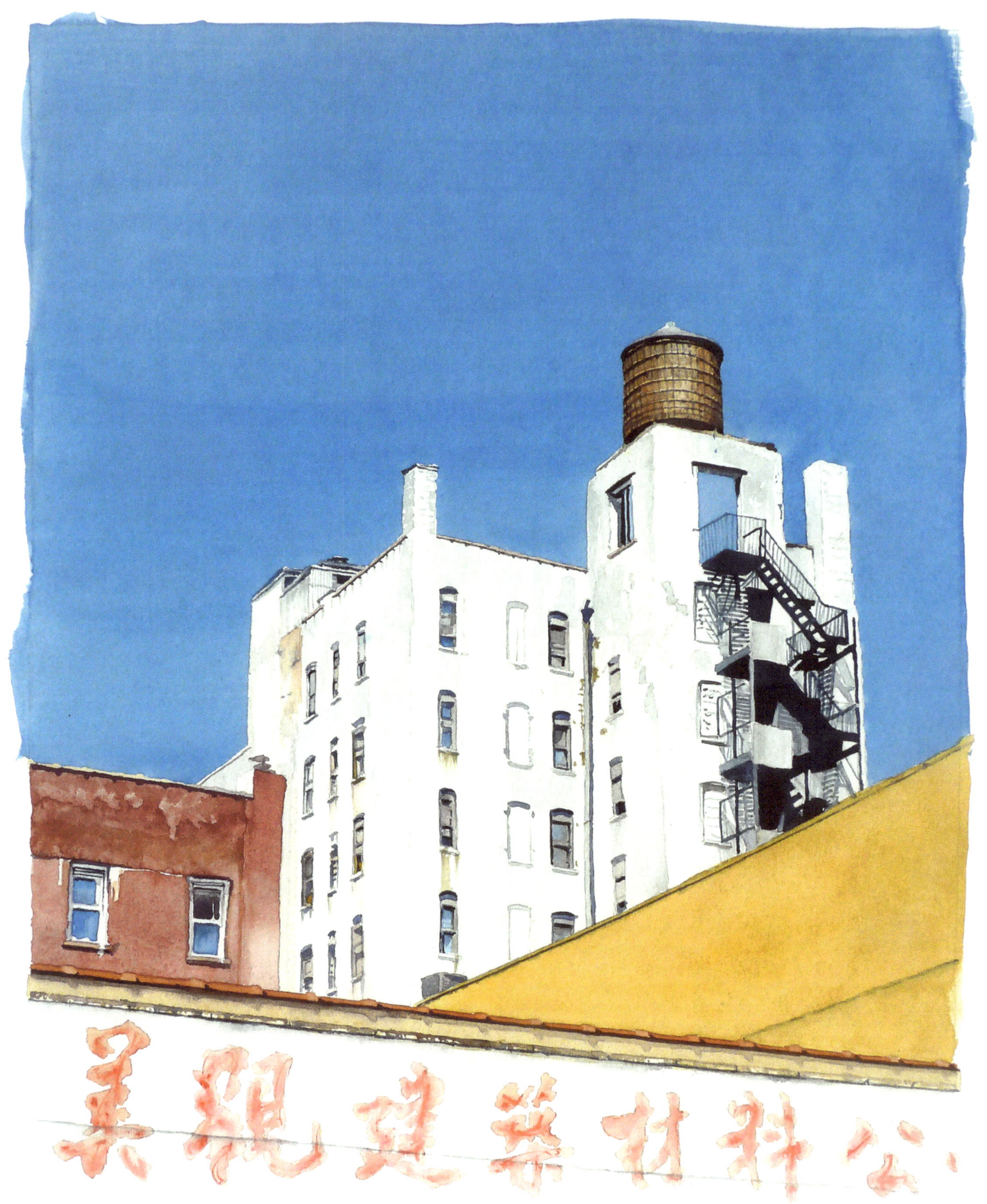
吳親建築材料公

This building isn't here anymore. This painting is here. What the painting is of, has changed. The buildings depicted, have changed and are not what they were. Lifetimes have meandered through the rooms and various steps were taken at different times across the wrought iron with hands holding the railings, the expanse looked out upon, in fleeting moments or in thoughtful measured observations. The people who passed through the doorways have their own stains, the paint has peeled, the plaster has caked and sloughed off. All the windows have had their share of light, fair and not fair, some, maybe one will still be intact without a crack, perhaps more than one. The meaning and the function is intact despite the damage. This is how things retain meaning through cycles upon cycles, not without marks and wear.

When I looked up and saw this years ago, I saw the effects of time upon myself and this stolid structure of bricks, paint, cement. Drain pipes, the sinus, obstructed in places, not entirely clear. A doorway no longer in use, passages so relied upon, retired from a once vital function. How many sun-filled afternoons did this rooftop take for granted, how did the tar paper fold and buckle when the sudden demolishing began. It's just tearing down, rebuilding and tearing down again. It's just another building.

By recording the images of time passed, never recaptured except in these pictures, I save myself from being demolished. It wasn't that long ago when it was all so new to my eyes, so unseen.

Every day I make a mark, not as a replacement, but as one more element in the body as a whole. I must let what is done fall back. To paraphrase the ancient philosopher Heraclitus, a person can never walk into the same building twice, it's never the same building and it's never the same person. I am part new and part echo, the body has worn away but the voice remains.

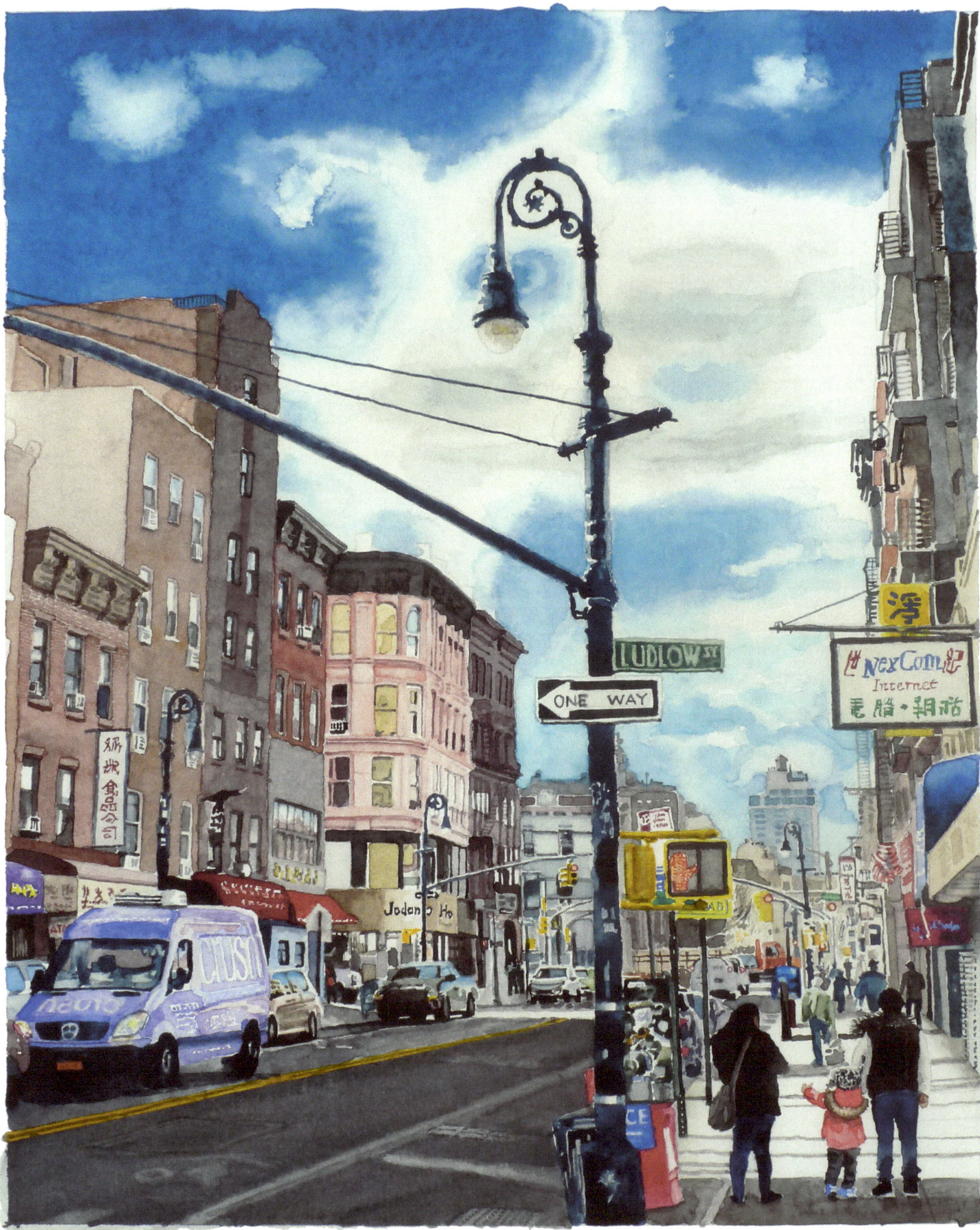
LUDLOW ST
ONE WAY
NexCom
Internet

Some streets on the lower east side are the ones you hear about most when this eclectic neighborhood is mentioned. Orchard Street, Grand Street and of course, Ludlow Street. All the streets everywhere in the city have personality, history and an unmistakable feeling. Always my first wonderment when walking on a street is, what if I lived on this street? What would my daily routine be? What would the weekend be like, or a weekday? I recognize the signs of frequent use and the cloistered nooks of inactivity. What gets paid attention to, and what doesn't other than the close attention I am paying at the moment. The least noticed aspect should be noticed. Everything else is there because of it. The awning on the store that has closed will be replaced but for now, it is quite there. It makes part of this painting and this painting will not be replaced.

Some people experience the city for a short time then are replaced by others also for limited periods. Some like myself, have been here for most of a lifetime. We observe the replacement of others, things and places. This creates the experience of a constant transit around us. Like living in a train station. It is a strange permanence within the temporary condition of the landscape. The things that remain have special significance, simply because they are still here. We collect things and keep them in our apartments so that the unique thing, along with the unique moments and feelings emanating from it, can be preserved in our relatively permanent universe. Emphasis on "relative" regarding that little universe, but all things small are also big. All things in transit come to rest periodically. It's big, it's small, it's here, it's gone, all this variation and transformation is exhausting, but it's also the city. That's why I stop, and breathe and look around. I try to notice everything.

Children have a monopoly on wonderment. They have a zeal that is not possible in adults. They are the proprietors of excitement and rent it to adults at an exploitive rate with a short term lease. The only way to own it is to be a child again. That means somehow completely surrendering to your impractical hopes. Our memories of mistakes and bad judgment offset our zeal. When the lifespan of our memories exceeds the lifespan of our dreams, it is difficult, possibly impossible, to recapture the abandon of the little wiggly kids.

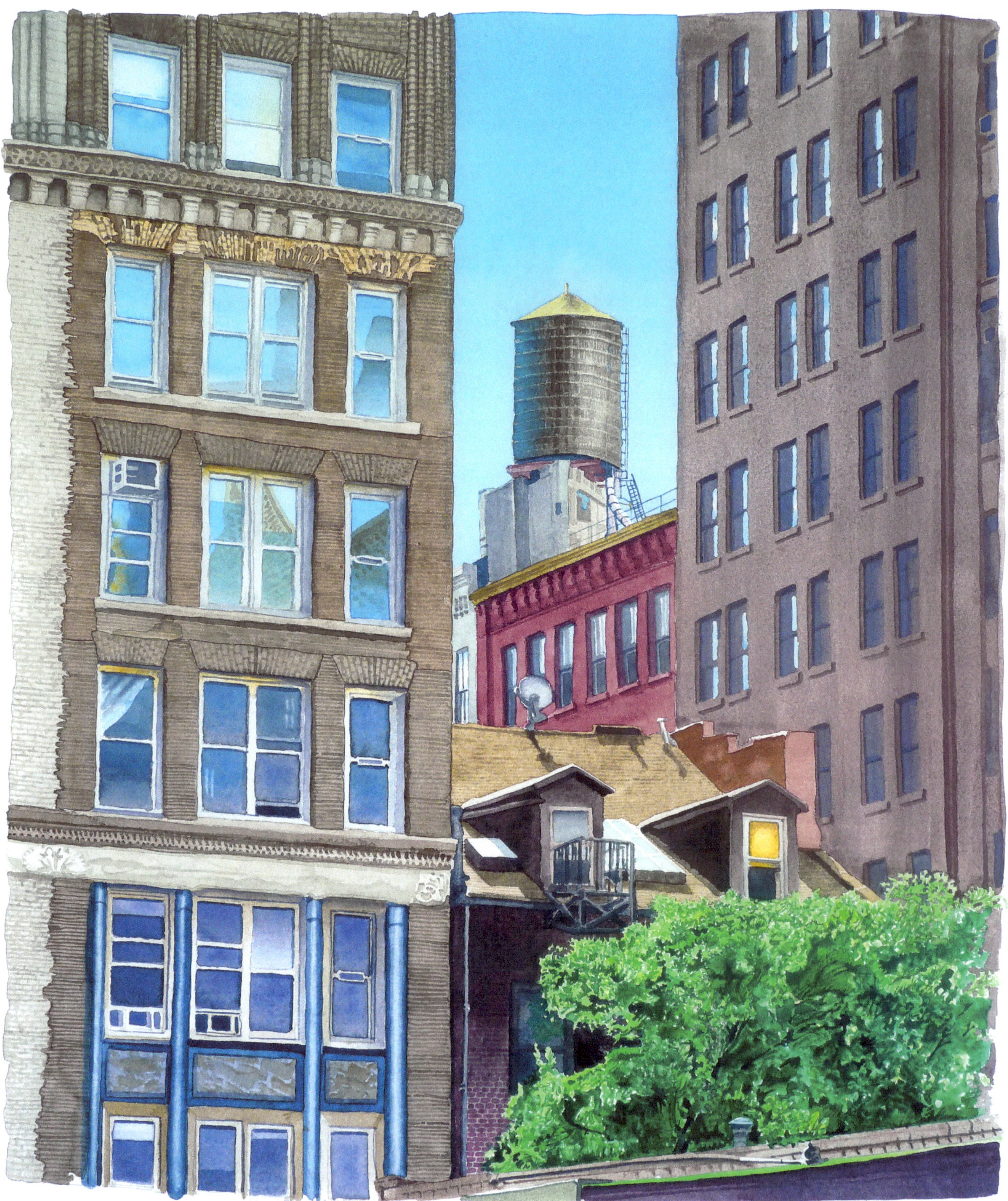

The refuge. Pick any window and it could be that. Whoever decided to go out and get a yellow shade lives in a cloistered place with a skylight. Other lives go on around but this one cries for attention. It's probably not the most remarkable, but our cultural thinking is always focused on the greatest or the highest, which I find stifling. After the competition, I will be the one that gets sent home. How could that be a bad thing? Home is free from judgment, it's the safe place where you can do what you want or what you need. There are so many windows, safety in numbers. The irony of the city is the protection of anonymity; there are so many we can go unnoticed which is what some of us want, others not so much. You can have both. Blend into the grid of spaces, and stand out with a yellow shade.

What does it mean when the environment is reflected back to us as a distortion. The sky is before us but our windows reflect the sky behind. It could be that our view of things and our reflections will always be a distortion based on the uniqueness of our construction. Like glass, it can never be perfect. Clear more or less, and that's the *good enough*, always anathema for the perfectionist. Here I will not make a sweeping statement about perfection because it is a yoke I bear. I have too much respect for the conflict. The struggle to create perfection creates an imperfect but transcendent result and the question comes up, how could something so imperfect be so right? One who struggles with exactness fears this enigma, to let up is to relent, to relent to the inferior. The slacker puts down the brush and says good enough, the neurotic perfectionist agitates the surface until the vision is dead. Somewhere between cold discipline and gestures of the hand, led by a nearly imperceptible sway of intuition, lies a window into a transcendent universe.

I choose to deploy both as a technique. I'm going for a clear uncontaminated interpretation born of intention and the surrender of intention. This is a dance of holding on and letting go at the same time. Our inclination is to use our skills to leverage our efforts but we can be dragged down and under with an obsession for control. Control in its most effective form knows when to surrender control. It's maddening, it's giving up yourself to save yourself.

When I look out over the sprawl and I see that elusive moment with all the surrounding nuance and detail, it is not myself that I see, it is myself that is seeing. I want my interpretation to be bigger and more inclusive than my limitations allow, so ultimately I let it have its own life. It is a work of art born partly of me and partly of its own. Then I know it is other than me, it is itself.

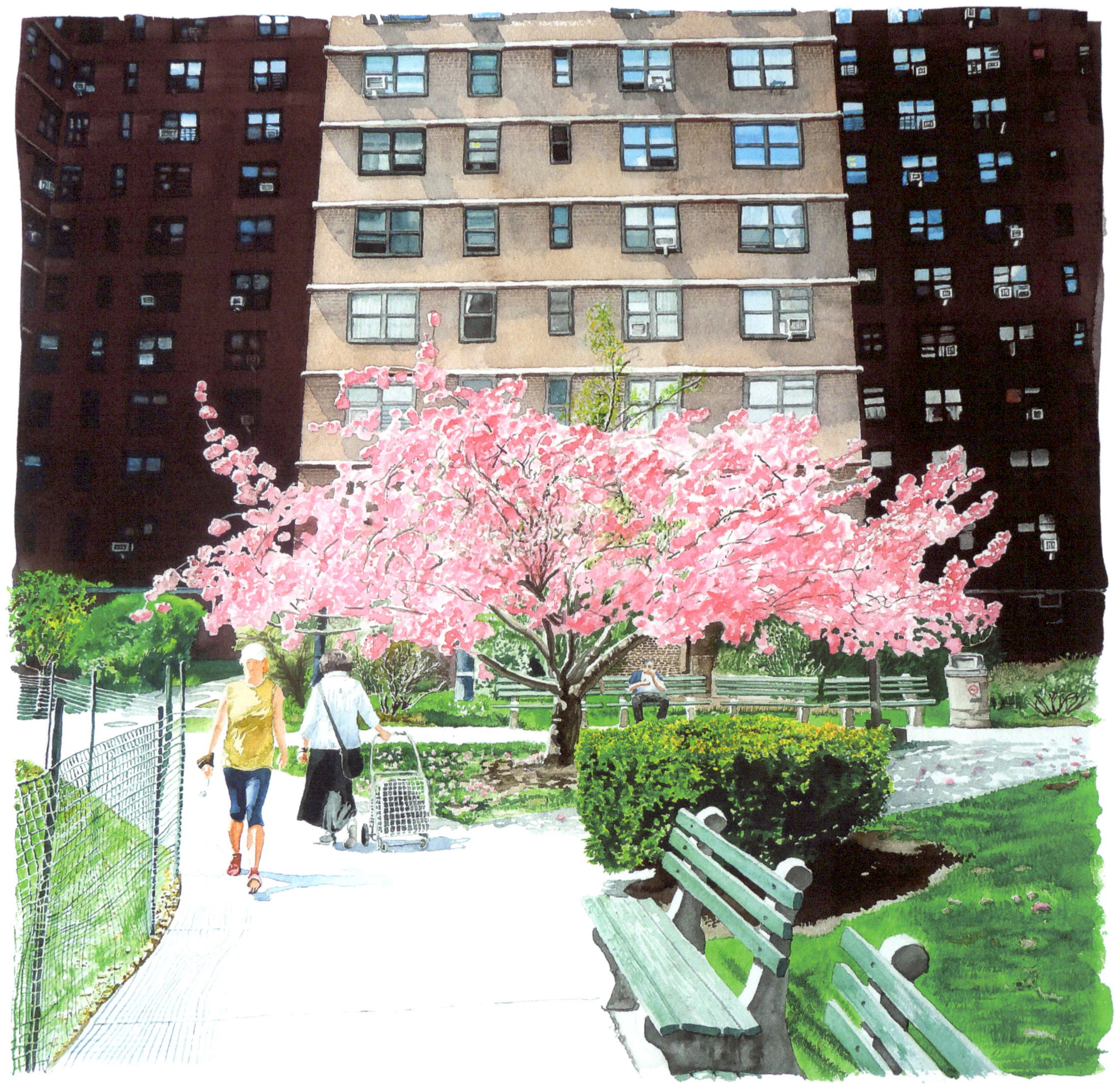

Springtime feels shorter than winter which is an understatement. Shorter than summer but less so. It's one of those vibrant seasonal moments that come as a surprise and leaves like an afterthought. The sunlight is sharp and shines extra color in the shadows. Bright chroma shoots out and fades like fireworks.

I pass through it like a street fair feeling the nuance and spectacle knowing it will be gone tomorrow. A neighbor might show a rare and infrequently indulged part of themselves and say hello, a notably positive chink in otherwise dour armor. People are here for diversity but are protected from it also. Once I was talking with a relative who lives in a very small town and they asked me how I could live here. "You never know who you are talking to!" "That's right." I said. "Exactly."

I paid for art school by working in Italian restaurants. There was an old Italian chef who started an employment service, his clients being all the places where he had worked or knew of. I was given his card during a desperate confessional moment with a guy at the Y. I went to the employment office where a stern figure with shiny black hair sat behind a big wooden desk. His name was Frank Messano. He set me up washing dishes first, then as a busboy in places all over Manhattan, Brooklyn and Queens. There were Italians working in these places obviously but actually more folks from South America. I was working in one crazy place where we all took a long break between lunch and dinner and sat around and ate and talked. There was an older guy, also a busboy around 50, Horacio or a version of that and he was from Uruguay. One day we were talking about disasters which comes up as a subject for discussion among restaurant staff periodically for some reason. He said that his wife, two daughters and mother in law were on a bus, along with about 15 other Uruguayans, going over a mountain to visit his cousins. The road was not in great condition, it had rained, the driver was *borracho* (drunk), and the bus slid slowly off over the edge for a long rolling plunge that ended at the bottom several hundred feet below. No one on the bus survived. He nodded and slowly moved his glass of seltzer water around in circles on the white cotton tablecloth. He said if I would sit with him over a few *cervezas* one night, he would tell me about some more of his disasters and we could cry together. I met Horacio through a rather obscure trajectory and learned something incredible. He was a happy laughing guy most of the time and I remember thinking dude, how can you be happy? But he was. He really was.

I live in a building which is a cooperative and everyone cooperates more or less. We have a tree downstairs that blooms crazy pink in spring. The blossoms cover the ground for a few days then the electric pink event is over. Some neighbors are preoccupied and reserved. There are those that say hello and those that don't. I'm intrigued by the ones that don't. You might say this is a city thing or an east coast thing, but I think it is a refuge thing. Some of my neighbors want to be here in the mix, exposed to the densely compacted proximity of extremely varied humanity but anonymous. I understand this. It might be that one can take in the intensity of the city's face as an observer but remain faceless and inconspicuous. This is freedom from expectation, interaction and potential social conflict. The conflict is inevitable, I like to interact sometimes and sometimes I regret it. Keeping a low profile is a best practice, we all love being here but as such different people. We can shop, we can go to the gym, we can sit and watch, we can remain cloistered within ourselves. We can say hello, or not.

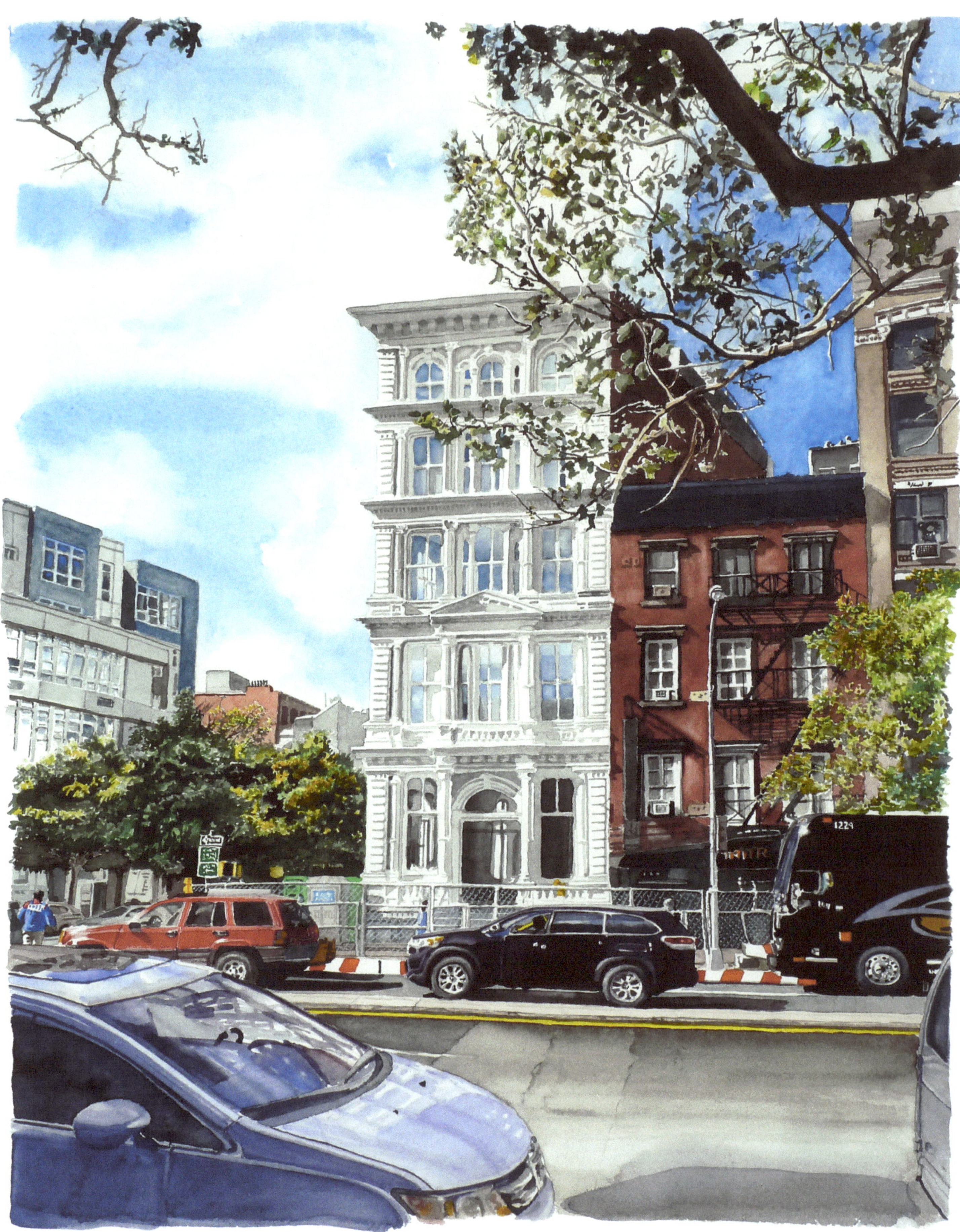

Evolution, construction, renovation, change. Growth, renewal, transformation, flux. If reliable consistency is what you seek, you will find it embodied in the dependable event of constant movement. It is the psyche of the city. There are things that indeed remain the same while everything around gets re-worked. Brick and mortar, steel and glass, rubber and asphalt, come down, go up and roll along. Red stripes and yellow lines are there to alert you, wire fencing might confine you, the light in old and new spaces could define you, and the maelstrom of structures have a life of their own. Some single segment in the patchwork might be your destination and it will not feel exactly like you imagined when you get there. Tread water or let the current carry you. Swim with conviction or float with distraction, the arteries swell and slack according to the mercurial municipal pulse.

One time, I passed by a swap meet in a parking lot on my way to somewhere. Folding tables held up trays of costume jewelry, kitchen stuff and old electronics that worked once, and maybe still do. There were some boxes of photographs mostly depicting the sky seen through branches and leaves. It was a theme apparently, and on the back of each was the location. The photos were from all over the world, but they were only of sky seen through trees and leaves. I was reassured knowing that if I woke up on the ground one day and saw the sky I would at least know where I was. The leaves would help but I'm not up on my dendrology so I couldn't really place myself exactly. I think that would be OK. Trees and sky put everything in a sort of stable context and then you can explore the options.

Living in a crazy morass of glass is filled with possibilities on the surface, through the surface, and reflected in the surface. Having direction is important of course yet I have learned not to be angered at inevitable detours. Roadblocks and re-direction are a pain but the sky and the light seem to always be there.

Seeing through a window into a room and then out another window in the same room gives you the experience of being outside and inside the room at once. It's the simultaneity of wanting to go somewhere, being there and going somewhere else. Being here is a way to be everywhere.

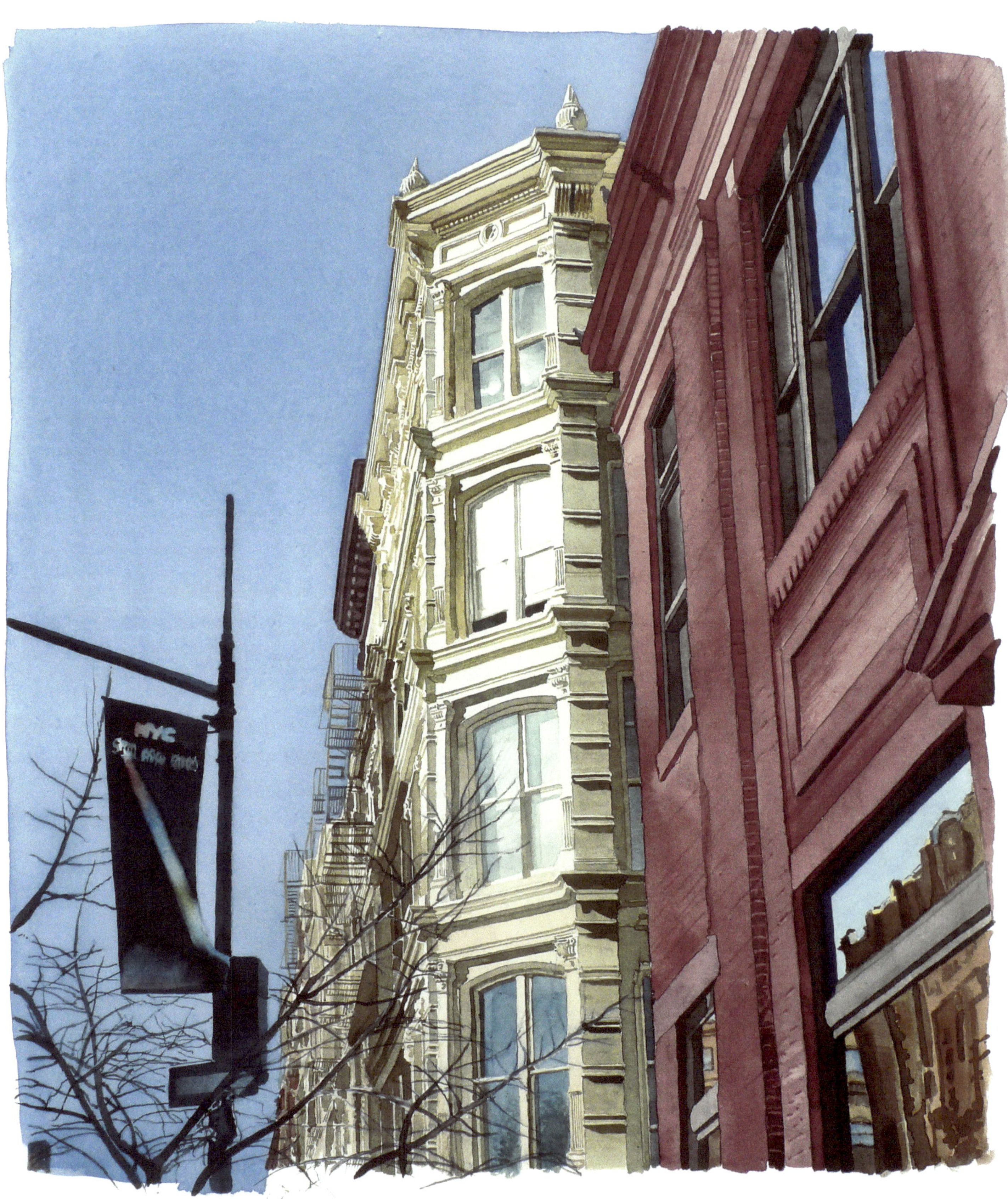
NYC

Soho and Tribeca as neighborhoods merge together in a way that has a distinctive nuance on late sunny afternoons in the winter. It's cold and bright with dark shadows. The buildings can have details that are considered unnecessarily ornate according to today's cost-driven construction standards and the modernist influence on architecture. It's always bothered me. Why can't we build things that are beautiful anymore? "Oh, but stamped out premanufactured glass and aluminum alloy monoliths are beautiful!" Not. I know it's not practical, but man, we really lost the beauty. We have what we made years ago, and you can see it when you walk along Prince, or Spring or down Broadway just above and down past Houston. Spacious open lofts, floor to ceiling windows, ornate details from ancient standards, you can live in one if you are wealthy.

You can sell high-end designer stuff on the ground floors, or up a few stairs. I guess it's posh, but I'm not posh and I still love the look of the old industrial spaces. OK, I can look, that's all. This also bothers me because my level of appreciation perhaps has more depth and attention to detail than the ones who can obtain it. The looking and longing at a warm luxurious window from the cold street and the empty pocket has been a theme for many artists throughout history.

I can capture the imagined potential of alluring spaces through bright sunlight without the rent or the overhead. I don't have to manage my assets or leverage my wealth. But I'm not really an occupant, nor would I really want to be, not really, maybe. Also, how could I pick? Which space would be the perfect dwelling place when the view would be of another perhaps better space. I have come up with the best escape from envy, capture what moves you, preserve it somehow, and bring it home. In your heart or in your room or both. Maybe they are the same. They should be the same or attempting to be so. I love all the rooms in this city, they are all in my heart. I don't have to choose except what to capture for now, I'll get to the rest at some point.

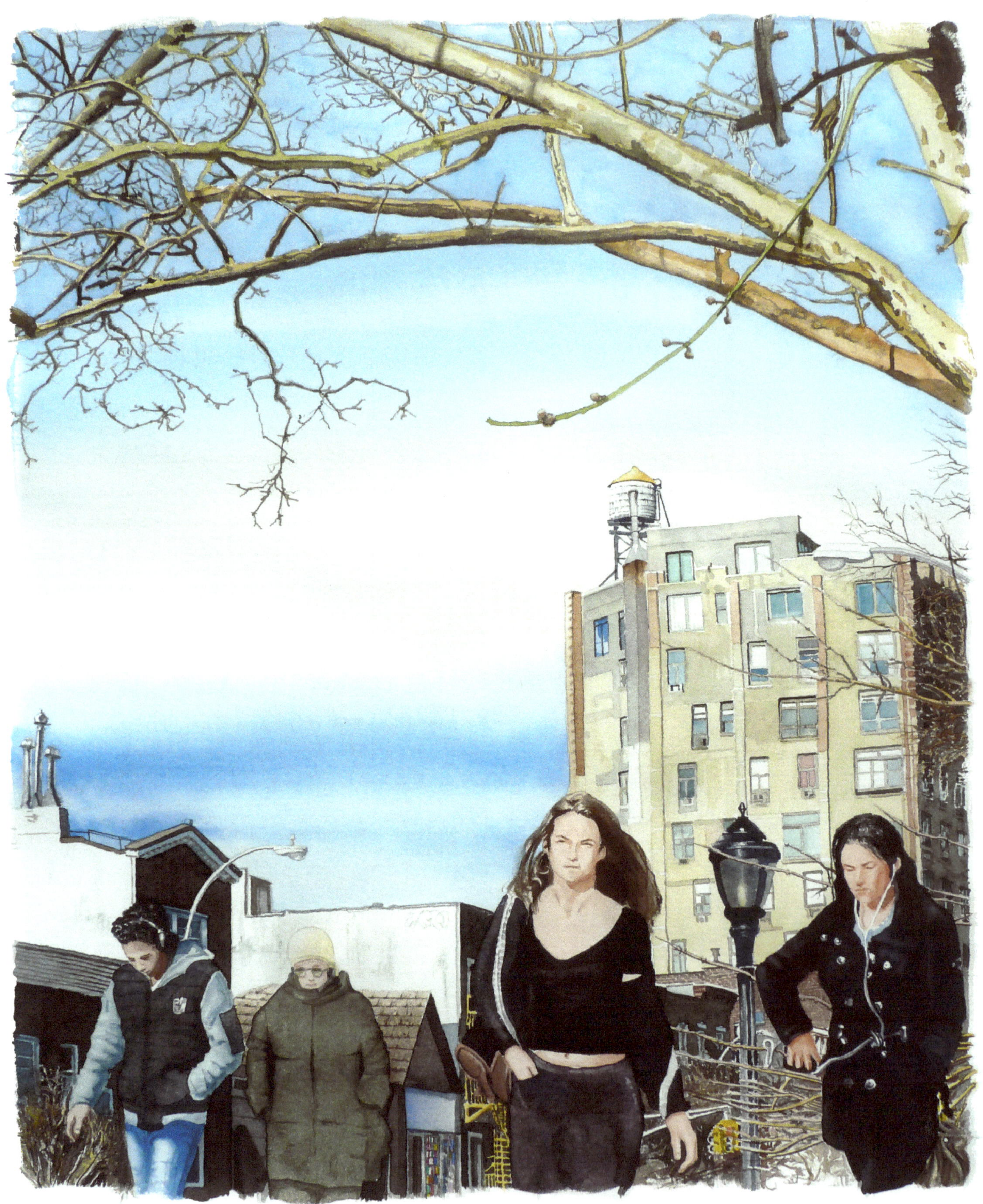

Stepping into a crowd is the practice of anonymity unless you start shouting. Even then if everyone else is shouting, you remain anonymous. When I first came to the city, I was naive, scared, brave, intrepid and moderately delusional. I was far away from home but in a place that felt like home if I could make it mine. I had to stake a claim. That meant stepping out, and stepping up. Also, I could just walk. Back then, there was a job for anyone who would work, a refuge for those who would remain here, and a chance to be something you couldn't elsewhere. There would be a cost, all the required mistakes and disillusioning scenarios, the acquired damage one has to sustain to achieve something of great value.

In this fragile niche that is our current culture, a way to avoid damage is to check out or exist in a form of electronic preoccupation. This seems like walking around in a kind of invisible Hazmat suit. I understand it to a degree, it's rough out there, but also it lacks engagement. Maybe it means that for a lot of us interacting with others in the immediate real time without any virtual boundaries is threatening. If we took headphones and mobile devices back 100 years in a time machine, once folks got used to them, would it be just like today? I'm thinking we are made of the same basic stuff that our ancestors were made of and it's just the environment that we are reacting to, not that we have devolved into a less socially connected life form.

Growing up seeing what we assess as important stuff on a screen via clicking, has produced a highly unrealistic translation of human interaction. This is not to say I am well adjusted just because I didn't grow up as a screenager. Perhaps it is a conceit but I like to think I'm processing my world with more authenticity. I can't say I'm completely well adjusted, none of us are, but I am especially out of adjustment regarding our device fixation culture, and apparently I like it that way. Things around me seem to be in the throes of an electronically induced downturn and I want folks to just look up.

I encourage trying to live free from the wire. I use it, I have to, and it's been a big part of me and my art but I seek to use it only when needed to more easily achieve something than without it. The end product, the final piece of paper that holds the vision, is created by hand. Perhaps you are only seeing it on a screen. A small one. I guess that's how it has to be for now.

If you are reading this on an actual page, holding image and word together as a book, it is what I have hoped for. Thank you.

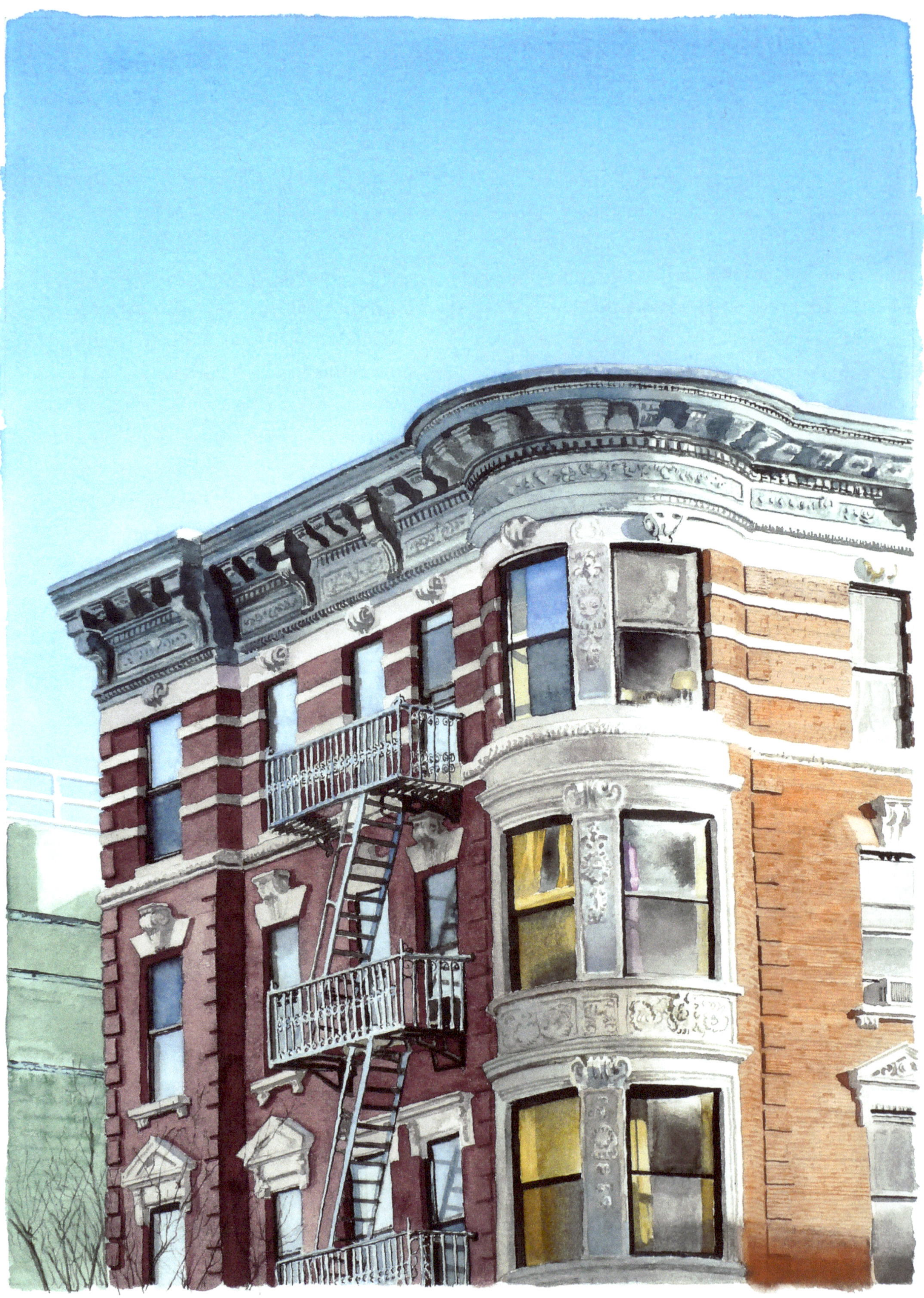

The top floor. Wealth can afford beauty but doesn't own it. I imagine myself living in all the spaces I look up at from the sidewalk, I try to imagine how I might have arrived there, the decisions I would have had to make.

Light from the window splashing across the table has the same glory on Houston and Clinton Streets as it does on Fifth Avenue. Someone has good fortune if they are living with a bay window. One way I can spot compelling detail in a building is when there are rounded corners. Our contemporary standards for new construction have abandoned the extra work and cost of finishing an edge with rounded style and detail. Will the turrets and circular windows be lost due to easier, faster and cheaper design?

The standards have changed, the majesty has been traded down for function and automated assembly. We have lost the work by hand idea entirely, we are an assembled society. Stamped out and shipped in, machines looking around at machines, or not looking, we know what we have become. It feels like I'm trying to capture the past. To somehow save it, keep it whole if only on paper, for those few who know what the majesty was.

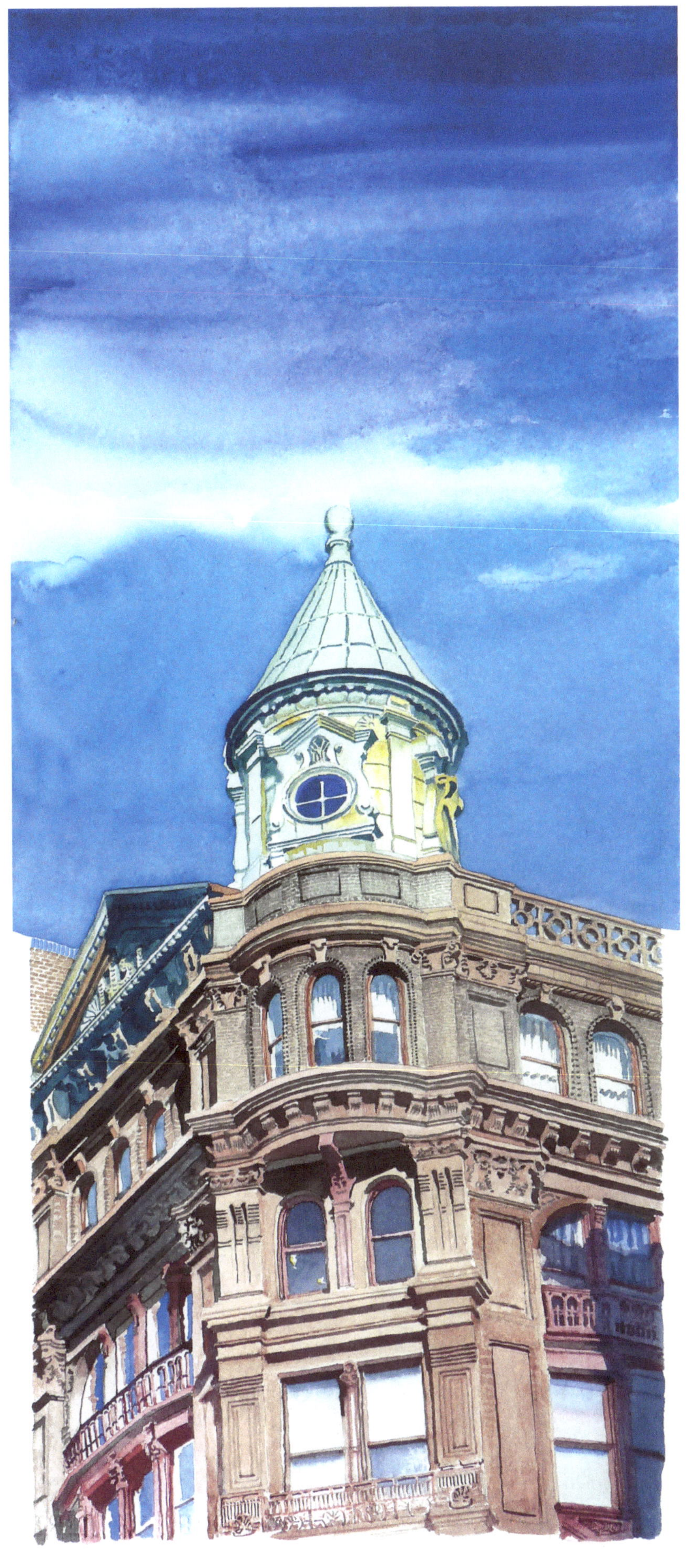

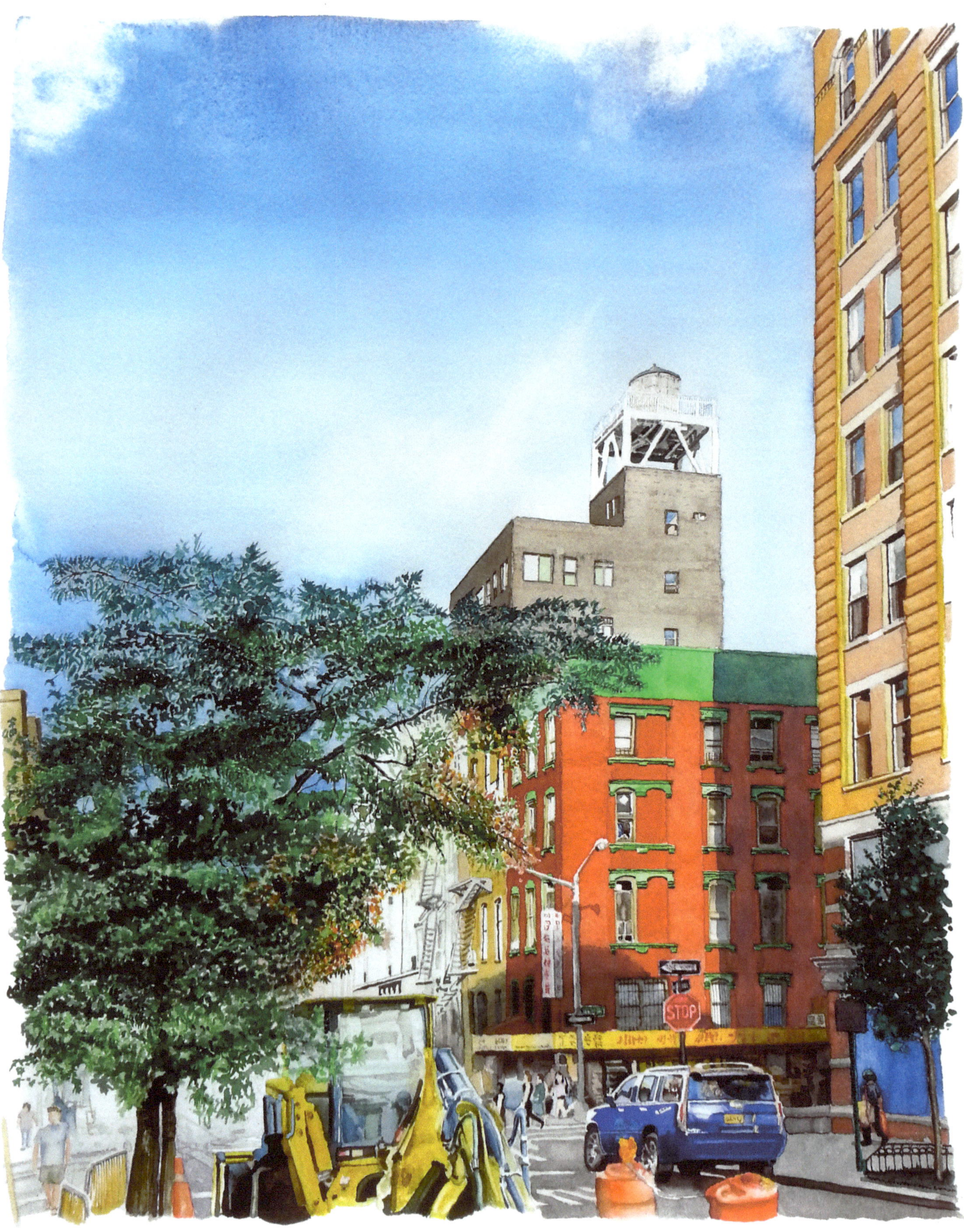
STOP

Leaves change independently to the proximity of bulldozers. They don't seem to care much if at all. I think they know that change is the medium through which all things are created and demolished and they know that all the earth moving construction utility machines also know this. Tall buildings catch a lot of light and they make expansive shadows and when you stand back, the contrast creates big depth. Trees and traffic cones are stable fixtures in the lush urban landscape, along with the folks on the street going somewhere. You can be looking out from a high floor then down on the street getting lunch, in the space of fifteen minutes. When I'm on the street and am blasted by the bold three-dimensionality, it's a giddy visual eruption. I'm usually on my way somewhere, so I look and walk not without being privately astonished even to this day.

Construction sites have never been described as majestic, magnificent or inspiring with any accuracy. It might have happened, but I'd have to see it. They occur with equal frequency along with the inspiring structures in the city and they are there to build, repair or maintain. It's like the elastic spandex braces and sleeves we have to put on our beautiful bodies eventually. Yes, we are still beautiful, but we have to wear this stupid knee brace. I go to a gym and engage in exercises that would equate with the activities and locations illustrated in Dante's inferno. If I don't, I will fall helplessly into disrepair. I want to beautify the bulldozer because it's needed and should have equal status with all the elegant stuff.

The need for repair hints at the inevitability of decay. As soon as things are put together, they begin to come apart. If you look at clouds, this idea will be evident as you watch. The construction and deconstruction of clouds happen within a much shorter time frame than buildings, streets, countries and civilizations, yet the evolution is ongoing. Entire generations of clouds begin and end in a day or an hour. Our city seems to be always beginning and ending. Paintings are a freeze-frame, they hold the world still long enough to really look. Later, you can look again, in case you missed something.

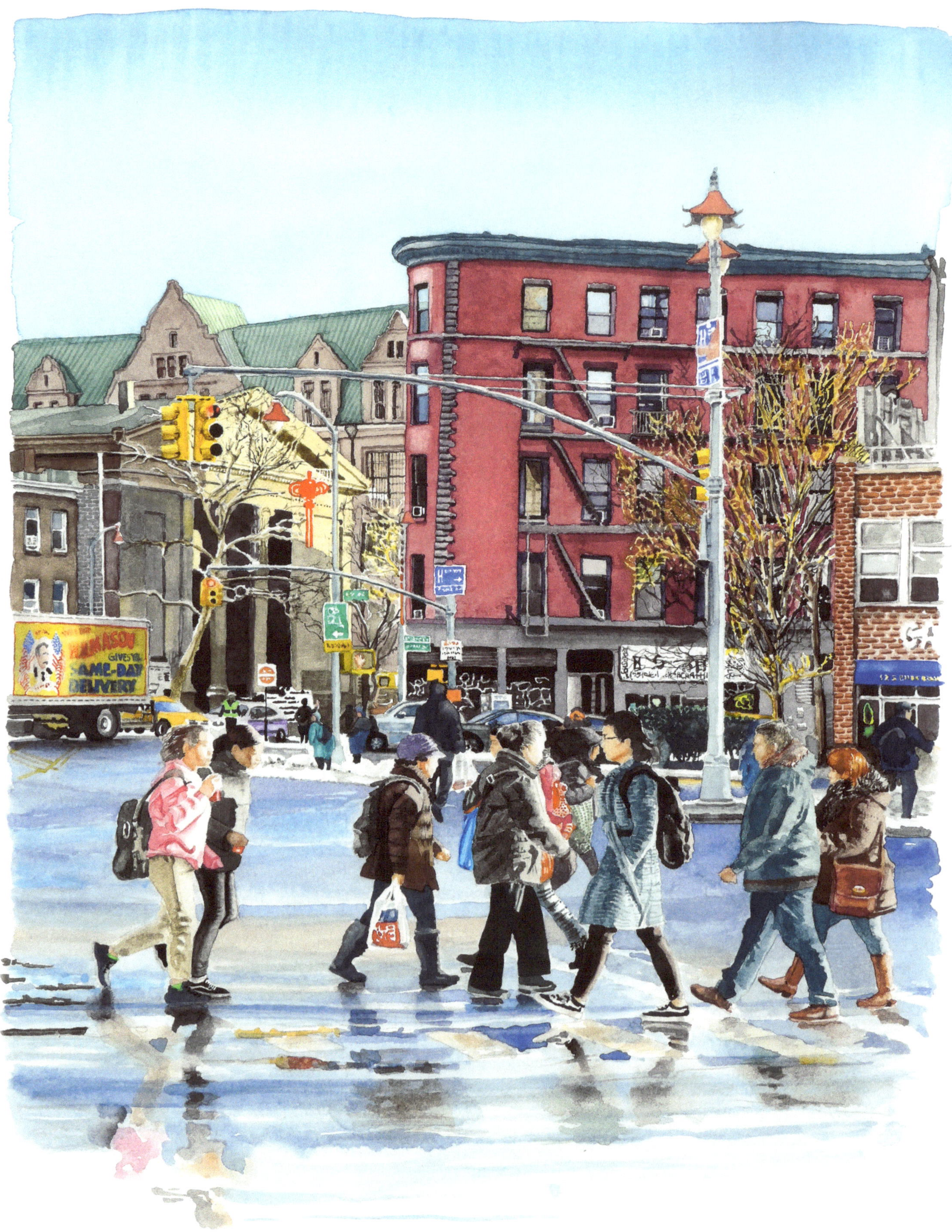
SAME-DAY
DELIVERY

The month of March comes along at the same exact rate of inevitability as all the other months, but a warmish day might make you think it jumped ahead in line. If there is snow and there often is, it melts and the streets are wet. They look blue. The sky is not just reflected back to us from windows. The color of the atmosphere is beneath our feet. The light at this time is bright, sharp, even a bit harsh. Deliveries continue to be made. Everything is still moving in this slow transition into warmer days and everyone carries around their stuff as always. Rooftops act as incidental sundials, hinting at the time of day. The feel of sun on your face and eyes is either reassuring or annoying.

The crosswalk in the city is like a walking bridge, the community of all ages cross over together despite quite different ultimate directions. It is a temporary convergence that points to our commonality within unique pathways. We are all going and will ultimately get there, with some probability. An element of unpredictability exists however, and often I end up somewhere unexpected. This should be expected. My perceived direction is subject to change, and I know I should allow for it. This is a bothersome risk unless remarkable things happen. All my emotional attachment to an imagined future is not necessarily a good investment. I like remarkable things, so I should stop trying to figure out where I'm going exactly and relent to a general direction with the caveat that circumstance likes to mess with the perfect plan.

Traffic lights are handy, but often slower in their pace of delegating permission than is comfortable for most. Proceeding without permission is allowed, but somewhat frowned on by anyone in charge of traffic wearing a fluorescent tunic. The best rule I have found for perambulatory city navigation is to be obedient with the occasional use of low-risk creative solutions. Often pedestrian anxiety is caused by an autonomic response to being late. Freedom from time constraint is a luxury, like having money, or not having it. Getting there on time is possible if you can afford it. If you're late, you were out of time.

Having enough money is of vital importance, but so is having enough time. We rarely think of free time as being quantified like this but now that I have some, I realize what intrinsic value it has. Taking the time to absorb this book is an investment, and I realize how expensive it is. Understand that it took a lot of time to create it, and now you are spending time on experiencing it. I believe it is worth it. Although it might not be evident or obvious on the surface, ultimately it has great value because painting and writing is spinning straw into gold.

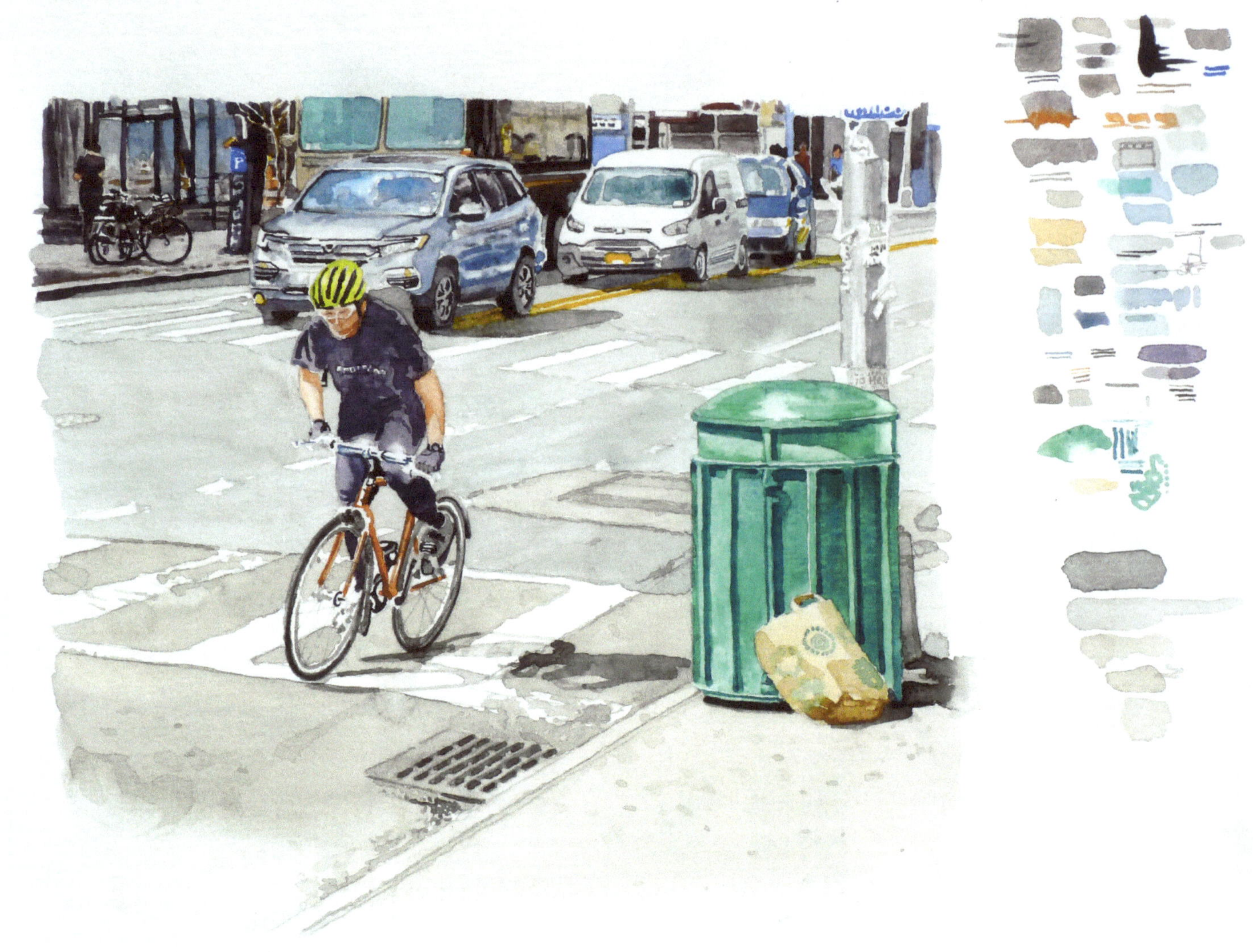

How many of us are really free. Also, what does that even mean—freedom. To act without prevention, to conduct one's life without restraint. What an impossible concept! In order to do anything, we are confronted with limitations. In order to breathe, we need air and lungs, this fact sets up a precondition for being in a body surrounded by air. Already we are limited at birth.

Where we started out in life, where we ended up, the work we had to do in order to have our latest interpretation of freedom, it's all a constraint. Somewhere in that balancing dance, there are moments of pure freedom, thankfully. For me, it is the marks on the page, the image I want to create with all its nuance and myriad messaging. I can't change the world of relentless endeavor, the striving of everyone around me, or the ways this is all conducted but I can capture its nuance and report on something unique about it. This might help us accept the condition and not react to it as if we were in prison.

A busy street in midtown is a good place to observe the personal universe of each member in this dense collection or multiverse of people. Separate and contained dialogues and narratives stream by like paintings in a gallery. City sidewalks and streets convey their contents in peristaltic motion, the individual uniqueness of the parts make up the intricate infinite texture of the whole.

It would be inaccurate to describe any single individual's experience as just wonderful, no one would agree with you. Although there might be a wonderful moment here or there, they would be offset by more prominent moments of toil and trouble. Expressions of concern, dread, or thoughts of preempting disaster are more common than bliss when walking along Eighth Avenue and 43rd Street.

Despite the angst however, something is floating just above the level of dread filled obligations, and I want to point it out. It's the indescribable persona of the actuality, the whisper of beauty that gets drowned out by the horns and shouts. It's in the essence of the rendering, that's one place you can find it.

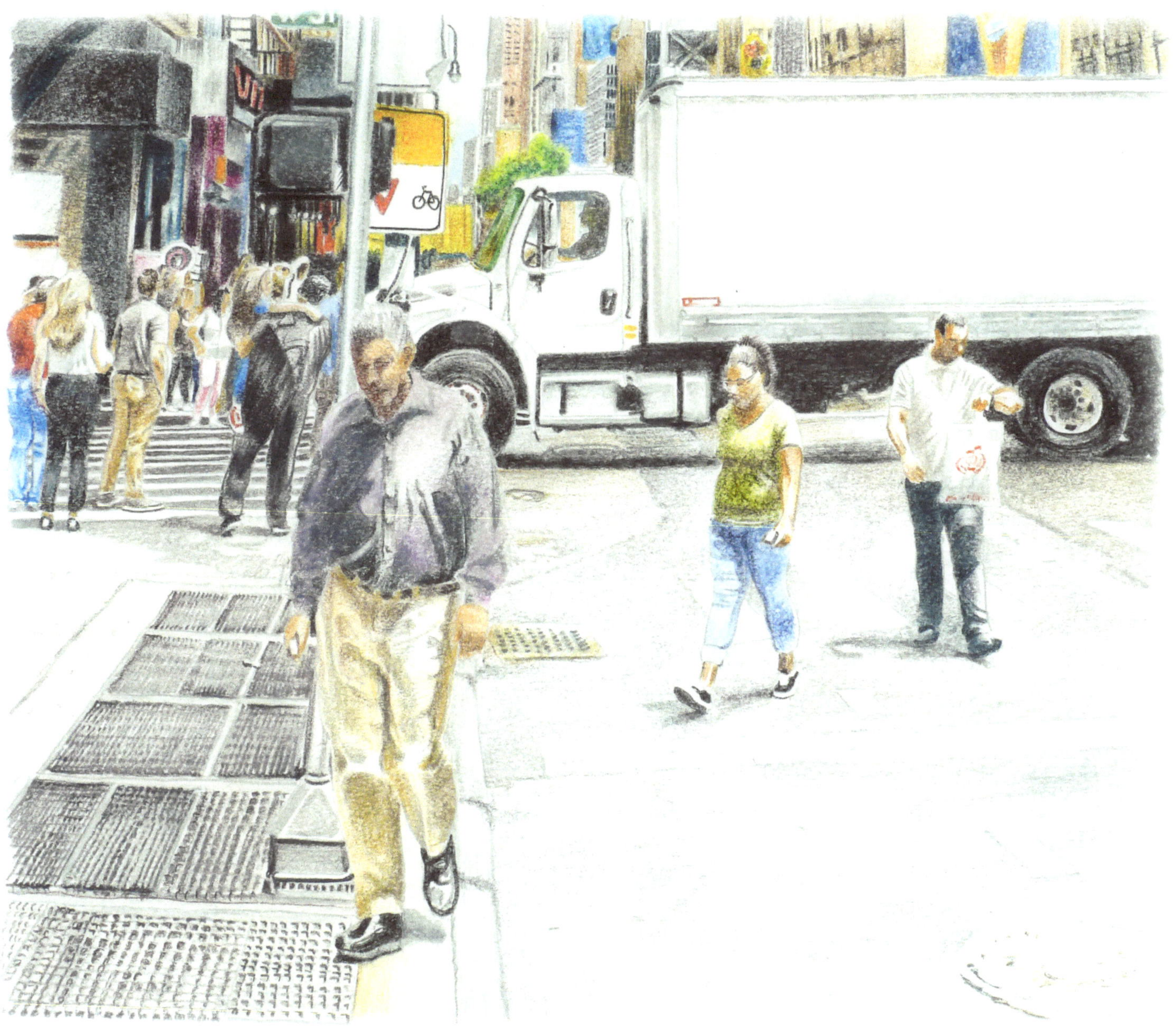

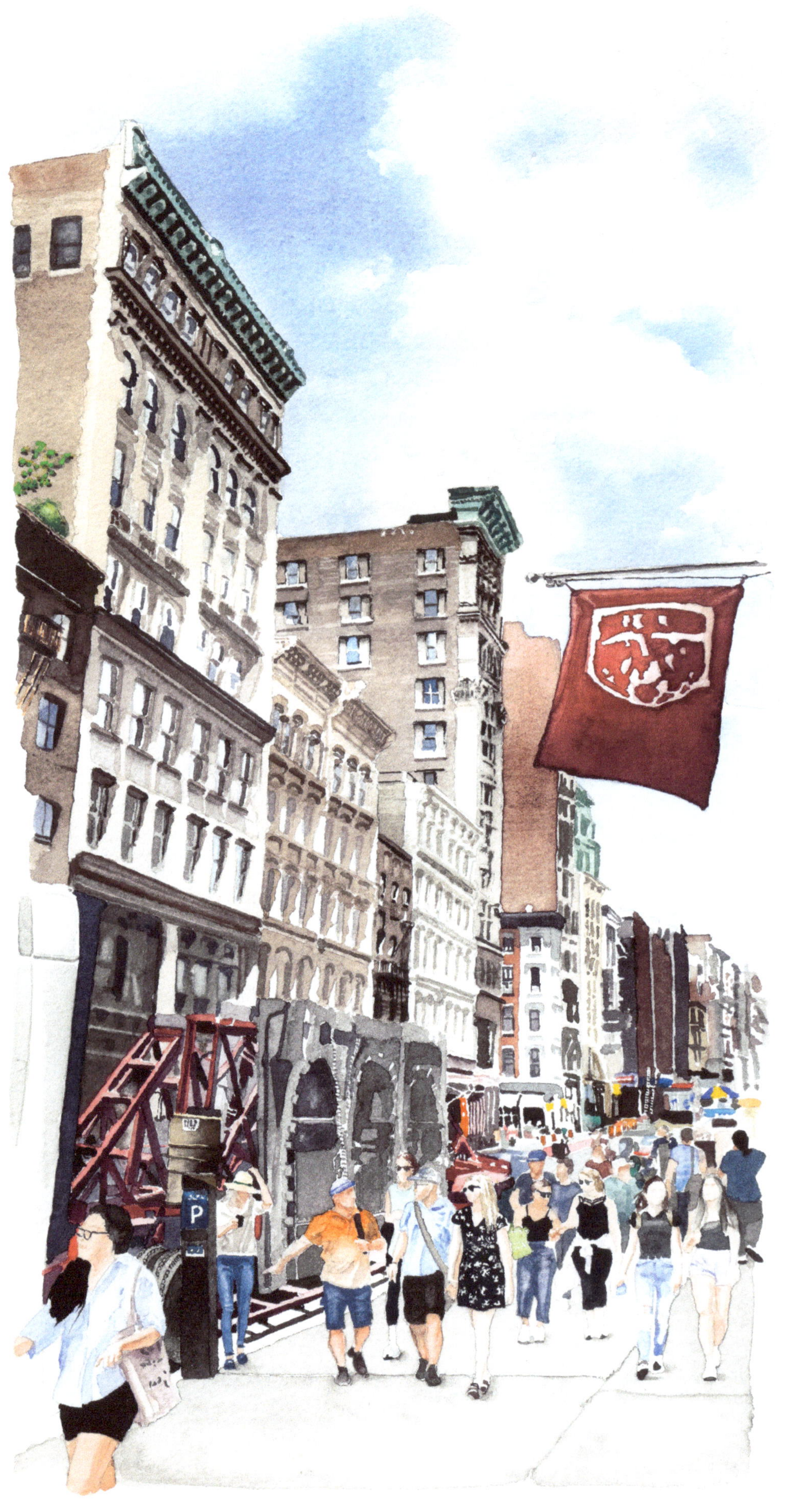

Taking a breezy stroll down Broadway might put you in the mood for watching other people buy stuff. This is better than buying stuff yourself and also cheaper. You can buy something, and that spontaneous purchase may knock around a closet for years and then surface and remind you of that day. The day you wanted that thing, and it was completely real at the time, unlike now which is you looking through a window into back then, via this thing you bought which seemed like a good idea at the time. You captured a moment in your life that is a record. You could even put it on, but I doubt it still fits. That's OK because you have grown since then.

I pulled a book off one of my shelves this morning and looked at it again for probably the one thousandth time. It is a collection of pen and ink drawings, some dip pen, some ballpoint, some pencil. It is an obsessive sequence that tells a story of tragic transformation and the technique is exquisite. The drawings have compelled me periodically and consistently and haven't failed the test of time. Some Scandinavian artist made this book and I got it cheap because there were so many extras that didn't sell. It might be one of the most inspirational books I have ever acquired. It wasn't a best seller, or prize-winning, or required for instruction in art schools, or even profitable for the artist (I'm guessing). I have kept it with me and looked admiringly and with some awe even now for all this time. I will always have it and re-experience it.

I'm just one cell in the multicellular organism of humanity soon to be absorbed and replaced. My book of paintings will most likely not be preserved in amber. Fossils have great meaning for the ones present to observe them. Is it the fossil or the observation that has the meaning? Is the relevance of the observation contingent on the relevance of the observer? These questions and the most certainly vague answers are the inspiration for me to make fossils. This activity is risky because the point is preservation and I'm not keeping my paintings in a tar pit. Hopefully, they will be preserved for a lifetime or more after mine.

Making fossils is an odd practice. People have made time capsules, but the making of fossils seems to have been mostly unintentional. Mummies are an intentional form of fossil making I suppose but I think to qualify as a true fossil you must be created by arbitrary circumstances and events.

My work can only become fossilized by some unpredictable event. I can't even imagine what it could be because that would invalidate the category of true fossil. I still have hope regarding my fossil making because so far, my life has to some degree turned out unpredictably and therefore so will be my fossilization. I have read about the frozen man and he might be a true fossil because his preservation was entirely unintentional. We don't know actually, that he didn't intend to become a fossil, it would have something to do with his grasp of such concepts at the time. Suffice it to say that even a fragment of fossil awareness by the frozen man would have been unlikely.

I am creating an incidental record. Recording what I know with an eye toward revealing what I can only guess. Ancient artists were looking forward and drawing on their powers of intuition. Navigating with the sextant of mystical perception along with reliable timeless technique is how I am becoming an ancient artist.

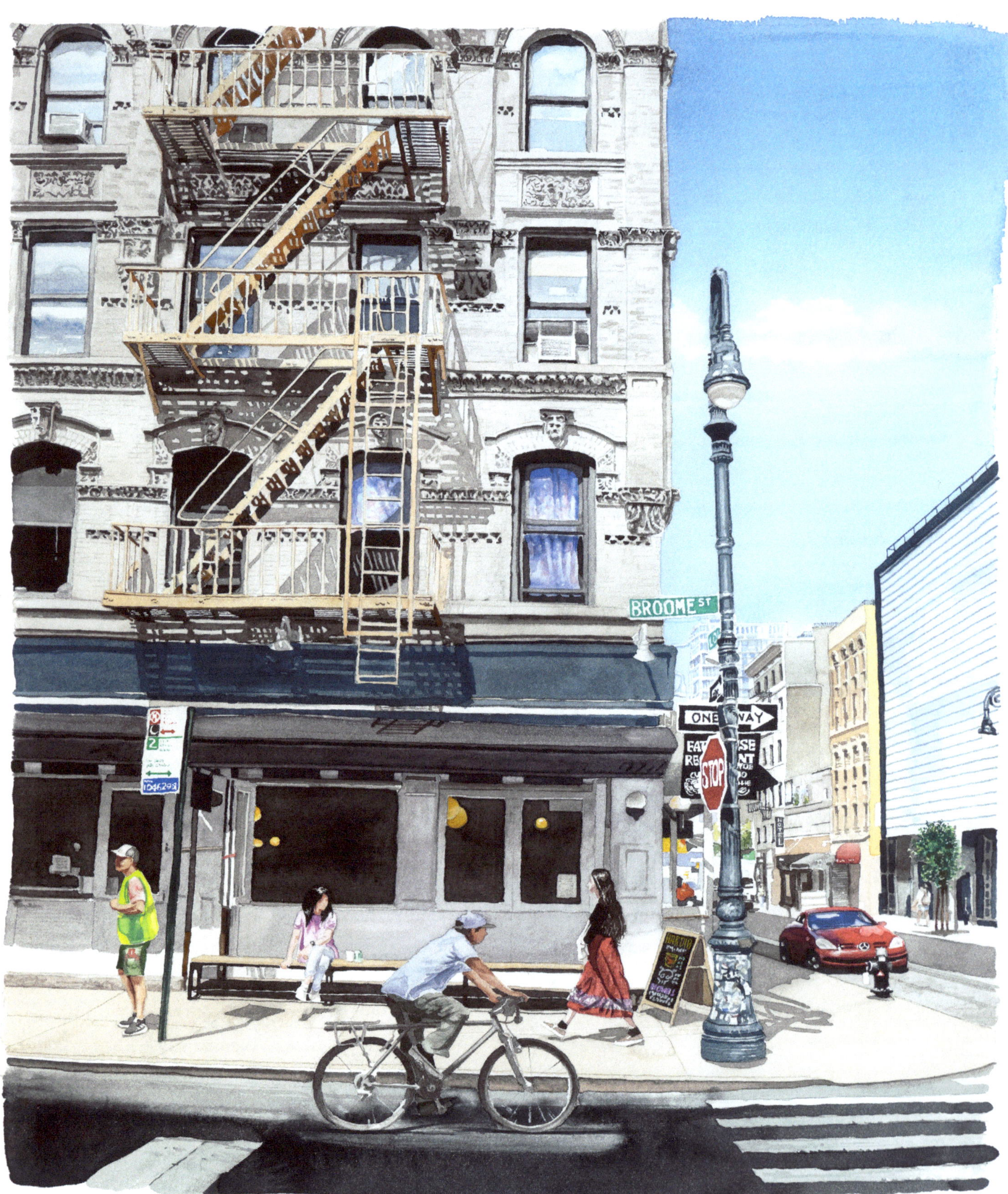
BROOME ST
STOP

Broome Street. I live around the corner, actually a couple of corners away. I walk past this intersection frequently and it makes me think about all the streets and all the corners in the city. None of them are the same. Street corners are like people. They often have a plethora of random information stuck in their brains. Stickers on our mental lamp posts. Information we thought we needed and can't peel off without tedious selective effort so we leave them there. We have our daily specials listed on our folding chalkboards. We are sitting on our benches watching everyone else. We have our maintenance endeavors. We pedal on to our immediate tasks, looking out for the best route toward long term goals. The streets are packed with options, most don't apply, but observing everything gives you the chance to pick what does. The street corner is a fascination with opportunity. It's a launchpad. The universe is before and all around us, and we can go there from here. A cascade of sunlight and shadow, reveal, conceal, and lay down a deep potential for exploration. Old and new are covalent organelles in the city amoeba. We pump along arterial streets bringing oxygen and endeavor. We can park for a while, and watch the pulse.

This is what I have discovered with all the years and months and weeks and days of frequent immersion in this primordial soup. I have come out of the water, broken through the surface tension, and am making strides on the warm pavement with thoughtful effort. There are capsules of inspiration all around, and I must consume them. That spark of light might be just a gum wrapper, but it shines so brightly. Maybe it's a coin or a key.

Not long after I went from immigrant vagabond waif to practical working stiff, I started really breathing the air of hope. I guess that's what they call the dream. Yet standing, sitting or walking past a street corner gives me a kind of hope not dependent on fortune endowed or hard-won. It is the kind dependent on certain freedom, not beholding to anything other than the virtue of choice. In the multiverse on Broome Street, infinite pathways are at perfect right angles to each other.

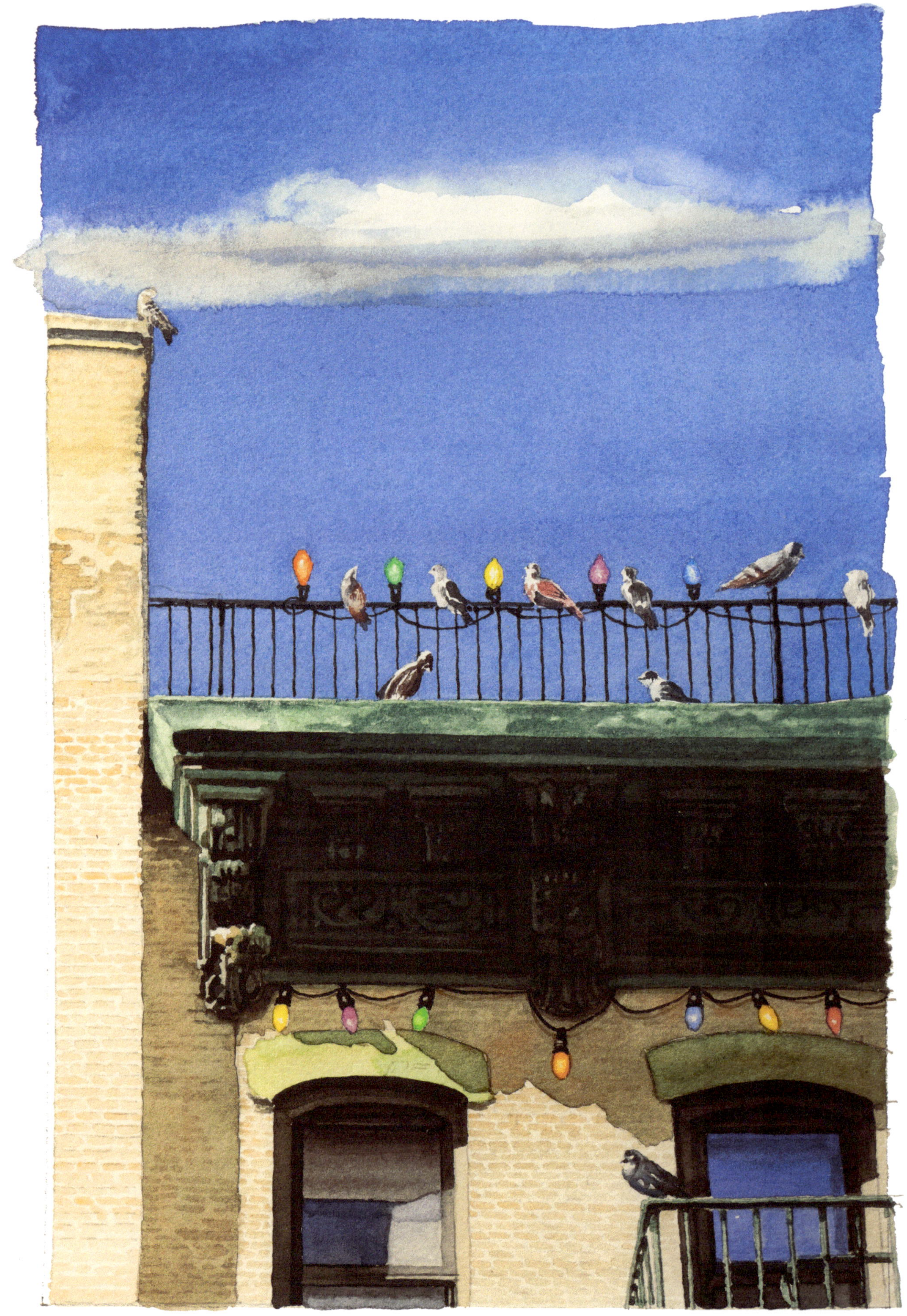

The moment and the essence, the fleeting impression, is what I have found myself still attached to after all this time. My home is where I want to be and when I'm walking and looking I try to find that shiny diamond in the rough snapshot that I can transform into the indelible cut stone of value. I suppose it should be like an end of the year celebration, with the celebration ending as well.

I have found a moment when the sun shines on the fire escape and the bricks behind. Bright moments without direct sun. Light on window panes, revealing the presence of worlds unseen. Lives I can only imagine. I can barely imagine my own life in its truest form, who would describe it? Using what language, what words, who would interpret the meaning of the words, what would be the cultural syntax, how would all the nuances be addressed?

It's late December, someone strung some lights on a railing, and our avian counterparts are bearing witness in a kind of distracted bird assembly. There is the detailed Gothic cornice stamped out of copper sheet with years of accumulated patina. Windows, railings, bricks. Lights. One arbitrary cloud, late to arrive, soon to leave. It's just a day, the planet's breath. I am here looking, capturing without restricting, taking my own breath. This has to be all there is to it. Then I can relax and just do this. Was that what all the fuss was about? Could it be that simple? I guess nothing is just one thing but one thing can be something. Here is that thing, here is my thing. Late to arrive and soon to go.

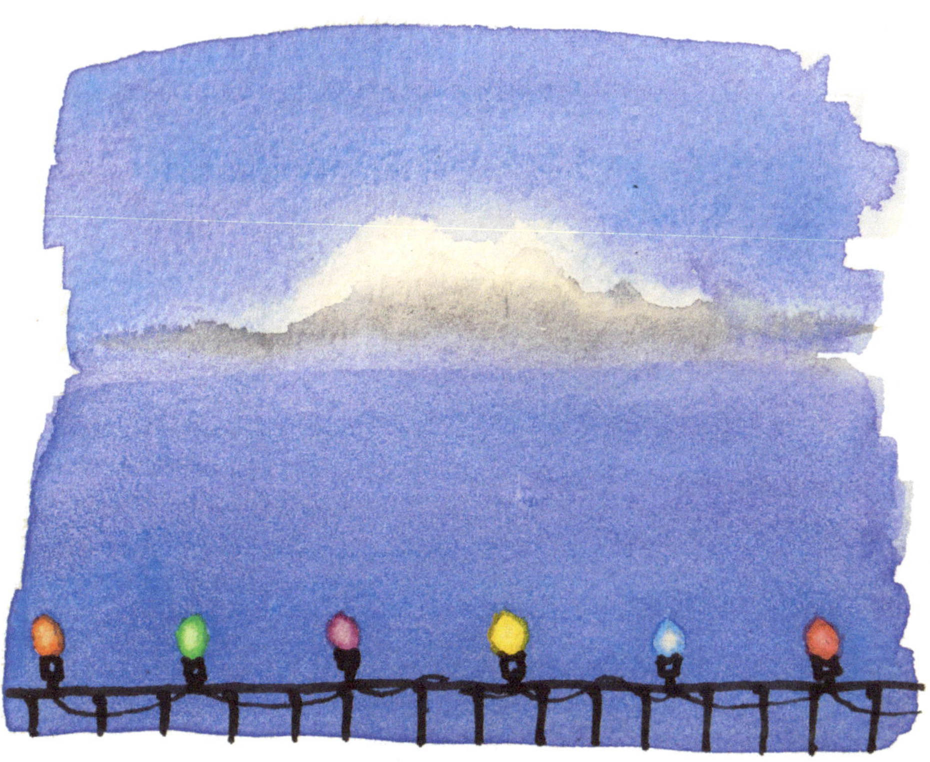

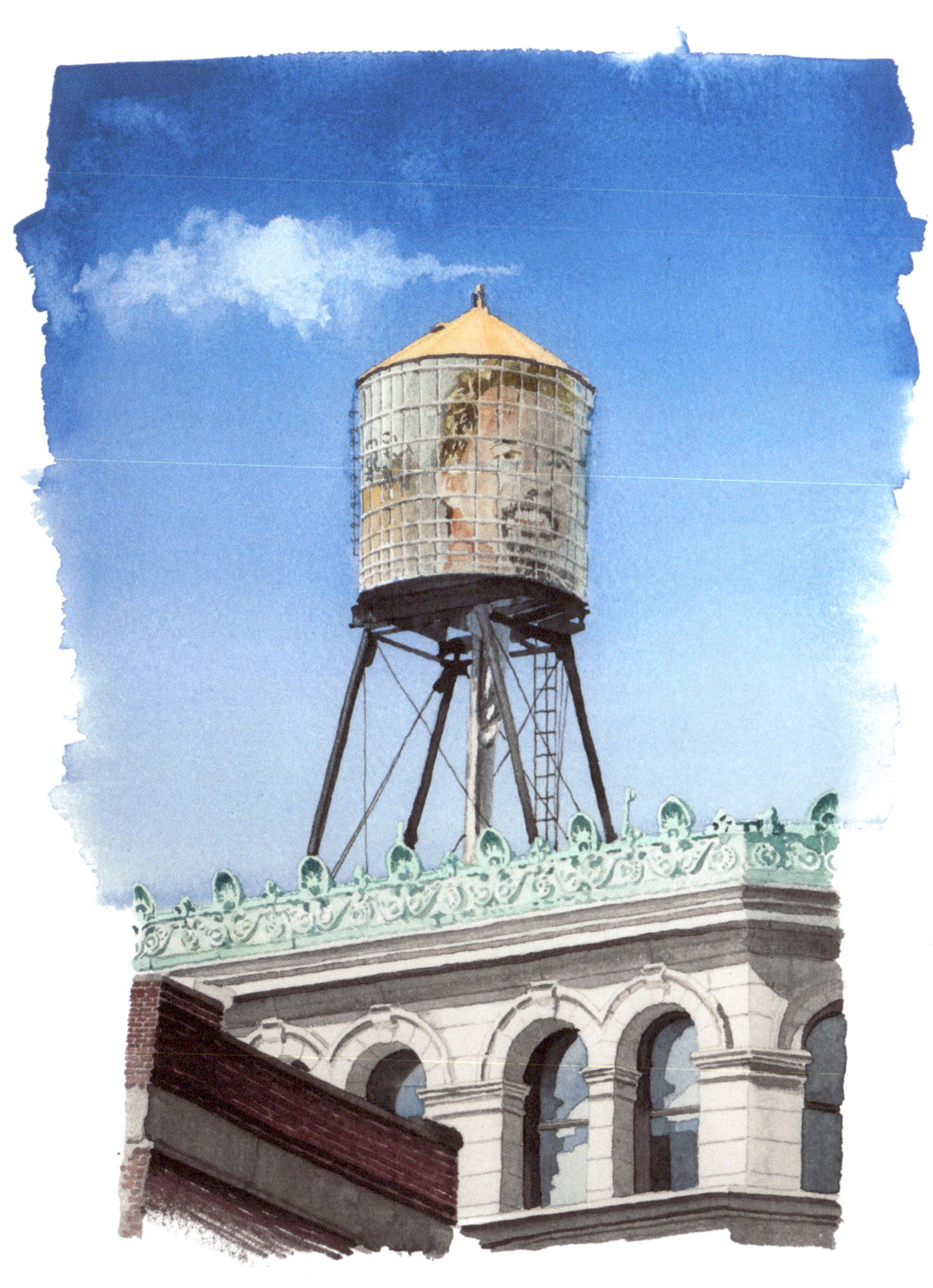

Alex Price is an artist, writer and painter.
He lives on the Lower East Side
of Manhattan, New York City.

CPSIA information can be obtained
at www.ICGtesting.com
Printed in the USA
LVHW070006061120
670806LV00019B/666
* 9 7 8 0 5 7 8 7 2 3 9 1 4 *